"Beautiful... want you...

Lance's words stunned Janie almost as much as his kiss had. She stared at him wordlessly.

"If you're honest," Lance continued huskily as he reached for her, "you'll admit you want us to make love. Go on, tell me the truth."

Much as she longed to respond to his touch, Janie moved away. "Aren't you forgetting a certain rumor about you marrying Penelope?"

"I can't believe what I'm hearing," Lance snapped, suddenly angry. "Are you insinuating that in the meantime I'm hankering after a roll in the hay with you?"

"You do have an understanding of some sort," Janie persisted, wishing all the while that he'd drag her into his arms and tell her she was wrong.

Miriam MacGregor began writing under the tutelage of a renowned military historian, and produced articles, books—fiction and nonfiction—concerning New Zealand's pioneer days, as well as plays for a local drama club. In 1984 she received an award for her contribution to New Zealand's literary field. She now writes romance novels exclusively and derives great pleasure from offering readers escape from everyday life. She and her husband live on a sheep-and-cattle station near the small town of Waipawa.

Books by Miriam MacGregor

Don't miss any of our special offers. Write to us at the following address for information on our newest releases.

Harlequin Reader Service
901 Fuhrmann Blvd., P.O. Box 1397, Buffalo, NY 14240
Canadian address: P.O. Box 603,
Fort Erie, Ont. L2A 5X3

Rider
of the Hills
Miriam MacGregor

Harlequin Books

TORONTO • NEW YORK • LONDON
AMSTERDAM • PARIS • SYDNEY • HAMBURG
STOCKHOLM • ATHENS • TOKYO • MILAN

Original hardcover edition published in 1988
by Mills & Boon Limited

ISBN 0-373-02931-4

Harlequin Romance first edition September 1988

CHAPTER ONE

JANINE MEREDITH frowned as she reread the letter that had arrived by the morning post. It was irritating, to say the least. She had watched the postman draw near to their house, and had seen him push mail into the box at the entrance to their short drive. Full of hope that perhaps one of her short stories had been accepted, she had rushed out to collect it—only to be faced by an annoying demand guaranteed to ruin her day.

Listless steps took her from the lounge to the windows of the glassed-in porch, where she stood gazing at the grassy verge across the road, and then beyond it to where the sea lapped the Westshore beach. The bay sparkled with blue brilliance beneath a cloudless October sky, while across the water a ship was putting to sea from the Port of Napier. However, little of the scene registered with her.

The stillness of her attitude caught her mother's attention. 'Is something wrong, dear?' Laura Meredith asked anxiously. 'You're not usually so quiet when the mail comes.'

Her words caused frustration to burst forth. '*Wrong?* I'll say there is. It's an absolute *pest!*'

'In what way, dear?' Laura asked calmly as she adjusted the massed blooms in a vase of freshly cut lilac. 'What is that letter?'

Janie gave the single page an impatient flick. 'It's from the editor of that Auckland sports magazine. You know I'm a stringer for them.'

Laura's brows rose slightly. 'That always sounds such a silly word to me. I know you're a freelance writer, but why *stringer?*'

'You can call it journalistic jargon,' Janie explained patiently. 'A stringer is a part-time news correspondent who covers stories in his or her own district.'

Laura sent her a sharp glance. 'Don't tell me they've rejected your last article, or whatever you sent them?'

'No, but they've rejected my reasons for not sending them the story they asked me to do.'

'I don't understand, dear.' Laura came through the open double doors that connected the lounge to the porch. She had turned fifty, and although there were grey streaks in her Titian hair she looked more like Janie's elder sister than her mother.

Janie sighed as she laid the letter on a round wicker table and sank into the chair beside it. The sun, streaming through the window, turned her hair to a shining mass of tumbled pale gold waves, while the troubled eyes she turned to her mother were as blue as the ocean depths. 'Didn't I tell you the editor asked me to do a story on that polo-playing wizard—that master of the mallet—captain of his team, etcetera, etcetera?'

'I don't recall you mentioning it, dear.'

'Oh, well, I suppose it was because we don't talk about polo these days.'

'That's true. It's all in the past.' Laura's eyes clouded as she gazed towards the bay. 'Polo now seems to be part of another life we once knew. But who is this man? Is he someone we met during those days?'

Janie shook her head. 'I'm sure I've never met him, but there was a photo of him in the paper last season. You know the sort of thing—Lance Winter shoots the winning goal.' The action-packed illustration had carried sufficient impact to cause her to remember it—nor had its principal figure failed to catch her attention.

'*Lance Winter!*' Laura's exclamation hit her daughter's ears. 'You *did* say—Lance Winter?'

Janie's eyes widened as her face jerked round to regard

her mother. 'Don't tell me you *know* him—that you've met him.'

'No, dear, he wasn't in the North Island when your father was playing, but we knew his aunt and uncle. Don't you remember Nell Abbott and her companion-help, Maud Perry who never stopped knitting? They used to sit and watch the matches with me.'

Janie's face brightened. 'I remember them, although I saw little of them because I was always busy taking care of the ponies.' She frowned as she cast her mind back to her father's polo-playing days. 'Didn't the Abbotts live on a coastal sheep station?'

'Yes, on a place known as Golden Hills. I presume you've tried to get in touch with Lance Winter?'

'You can say *that* again! I phoned him to make an appointment and was given short shrift. In fact, I was given a thorough brush-off. He refused point-blank to see me.'

'Really? I wonder why.'

Janie went on in an aggrieved tone, 'He was very terse while explaining that he refuses to give interviews to *anyone*. He told me in definite terms that he was a private sort of guy—that he doesn't want his thoughts, opinions or methods of training polo ponies splashed over the pages of some tinpot little magazine. The—the *confounded nerve of him!*' she finally exploded.

'He sounds a very strong-minded sort of person,' Laura mused.

'Rude and arrogant are better words. Really, Mother—I find difficulty in associating him with that gentle little woman, Nell Abbott—nor can I get over the fact of her being his *aunt*—to say nothing of the fact that you *know* her.'

'My dear, you're forgetting that her husband played polo, and during those days we knew most of the polo enthusiasts.'

'Well, at least those in our district,' Janie conceded. 'But why wasn't Lance Winter there?'

'I understand he was gaining experience on farms in the South Island. It was his uncle's death that brought him home to take over the running of Golden Hills.'

'You even know the name of the place—and there was I, having an awful struggle to find out where he lived.'

'Janie, dear—you didn't *tell* me. You write so many articles and short stores—you *know* you don't discuss them all with me.' Laura picked up the letter and glanced through it. 'Well, what will you do about this?'

'I don't know. I'll have to think about it. As you can see, the editor is asking me to make another attempt to interview the—the *wretched man.*'

'Do you feel you want to?'

'*Definitely not.*' The words came vehemently, almost as if she wished to convince herself on this point.

'Then make that fact clear to the editor,' Laura advised. 'In any case, what's so special about Lance Winter? Why are they so anxious to get a story about him? I'm sure there are plenty of other good players.'

'It's because he's an authority on the sport. By the end of last season, he'd reached the stage of being a top polo player, and since then he's played in overseas countries.'

'And that makes him a little different?' Laura smiled.

'On top of which, the editor would like the article in print during the polo season which begins in December—so will I please get myself into gear?'

'Players will be getting their ponies into training,' Laura reminisced sadly, her blue eyes, so similar to Janie's, clouding as she looked back into the past. She then sent her daughter a shrewd glance. 'I suspect you weren't too worried when he turned you down?'

'You're right, Mother. I've no wish to write about polo— nor is it necessary to explain the reason to you. Polo has too many memories for us.'

Laura sighed. 'My dear, I know how you feel. But you

can't allow the past to influence the present, and you must remember, it wasn't polo that killed your father, it was a massive coronary.'

'He was playing polo when it happened,' Janie reminded her, 'so I blame polo for his death.'

'He knew perfectly well that he had no right to be playing. He'd had *warnings*. He was being unfair to himself and to us,' Laura recalled bitterly. 'But that doesn't solve this particular problem.'

'No, it doesn't. It was quite a relief when he turned me down. I almost told him I couldn't care less—and now this rotten letter demands that I have another go at him.'

'Well, perhaps it's for the best——'

'How can it be for the best? Just listen to this! "A good interviewer is never turned away permanently by a first refusal." Now that's what I call a dirty dig, especially after I've explained that this man refuses to be interviewed by *anyone*.'

Laura regarded her daughter thoughtfully. 'I think you'll have to look upon it as part of your journalistic training.'

'You do? So how would *you* handle the situation?'

'First of all, I'd let the editor know I'm willing to try again. Then, instead of ringing for an appointment, I'd drive to Golden Hills to see the man.'

'You mean that I should just land on his mat from out of the blue? You're saying I should simply barge up and bang on his door?' Janie looked at her mother incredulously.

'It would stop him from slamming the receiver in your ear——'

'But it wouldn't stop him from sending me hopping sideways with a flea in my ear——'

'He won't do that if Nell's there,' Laura assured her with confidence. 'In fact, I have a better plan. I'll phone Nell and explain the situation to her. She might be able to help in some way. I'm also willing to believe that she'll want you to stay overnight or even longer. That's if you go there, of course.'

Janie laughed. 'Mother, you're the eternal optimist!'

'I am not—I'm merely talking common sense,' Laura declared calmly. 'And, what's more, I feel sure that Nell will be quite delighted to see you.'

'How can you be so positive?'

'Because she has always taken an interest in you.'

'Really, Mother—you exaggerate——'

'I do not. When we chat on the phone, she's always anxious to know how you are—and if you've become engaged to some nice young man. Oh yes, she'll want you to stay for a while.'

'You almost fill me with the hope of getting that article after all, but perhaps it's just because you know Nell Abbott. Can you tell me more about Lance Winter?'

'Very little, I'm afraid. I only know what Nell told me while we sat and watched the teams racing up and down the field, and that was mainly about their own situation.'

'Suppose you sit in the sun and rake your memory while I make some coffee? I want to know everything she told you—especially about her nephew.'

'My dear, it's so long ago——'

'Just sit and *think*. Drag up every detail,' Janie requested as she disappeared towards the kitchen. And in her haste she missed the speculative gleam in her mother's eye.

Why did she want to know about this irritating man? Janie found herself wondering as she placed coffee mugs on a tray. No doubt it was because he'd caused a problem. He was putting her on her mettle. Yes, that was it; he was a challenge. It had nothing to do with the fact that a newspaper photograph had stirred her imagination to the extent of making her wonder about him.

At the same time, she felt torn because she was genuinely reluctant to interview this man about polo. The game had too many poignant memories for her, and she feared she might break down and weep in the middle of it. A prize idiot she'd look then.

A short time later, she returned to where her mother sat in the sun, and as she placed the steaming mugs on the wicker table her apprehensions switched to the underlying interest that kept rearing its head. 'Now, then—tell me all you can remember,' she pleaded.

Laura sipped the hot drink reflectively. 'I've never been out to the place, although I recall that Nell said the homestead is quite near the sea. To reach it you drive in a southerly direction, then turn off to follow the road to the coast.'

'Is it far away?'

'Sixty miles or more. According to Nell the land was purchased by Lance's great-grandfather. It's probably a block cut from a larger neighbouring sheep station.'

'So it's been handed down from father to son?'

'That's right. Lance's father farmed it with Colin Abbott as his manager. Colin had married his sister, Nell, so the two men were brothers-in-law. They formed a happy quartet until the death of Lance's mother. Nell said she died after being thrown from a horse when Lance was about six.'

'Did his father marry again?'

'No. According to Nell, he never got over her death. And then some years later he himself fell from a dangerous part of the property that was edged by cliffs. There were rocks at the bottom of them, and it was thought that he'd hit his head, because he was dead when he was found.' She paused before going on thoughtfully, 'At the same time, there was also talk of suicide.'

'The poor man.' Janie's voice came softly, filled with sympathy.

'Colin Abbott continued to run the estate, and he also made sure that Lance gained experience on other properties, mainly in the South Island.'

'So that's why we never saw him at the polo matches.'

'Well, as I said before, it was Colin's death that brought him home to take over the running of Golden Hills. And that, I'm afraid, is all I can tell you.'

'At least it's given me a little about his background.' She fell silent until a question was dragged from her. 'Do you happen to know if—if he's married?'

Laura sent her a veiled glance. 'I don't think so—although Nell once mentioned something about somebody next door, or on a nearby property. I think I'd have heard if there had been a wedding.' Her tone became casual as she asked, 'So what will you do? Make another attempt—or admit defeat?'

Janie eyed her mother with suspicion. 'You wouldn't be pushing me out towards Golden Hills, would you, Mother?'

'I don't know what you're talking about, dear,' Laura hedged defensively. 'What on earth would give you such an idea?'

'The fact that you *could* be harbouring false hopes——'

'Rubbish! It's just that I *know* you miss living in the country, and I'm *sure* you'd enjoy a few days among horses and sheep and—and all the things that go to make up country living. Especially *polo ponies*——' She paused for breath.

'Aren't you forgetting something, Mother?' Janie asked drily.

'Am I, dear? What would that be?'

'You're forgetting to mention that Lance Winter must surely be the most eligible man in the district.'

Laura avoided her daughter's eyes as she said defensively, 'Really, Janine—I don't know what you mean.'

Janie laughed. 'Oh, come on, Mother—it's sticking out all over you.'

Laura became indignant. 'I can assure you I never gave it a thought.'

'You're telling an untruth, Mother.'

'Accuse me of lying if you wish, Janine, but you still

haven't told me what you intend to do.'

Janie's gaze wandered out towards the blue ocean. 'I'll do as you suggest,' she said at last. 'I can't possibly write to the editor admitting defeat—at least, not before I've made another attempt.'

'In that case, would you like me to phone Nell?'

'Yes, please—I'd be most grateful. I wouldn't dream of going there without her invitation.'

'Of course not.' Laura drained her mug rapidly, then went to the phone with brisk steps.

During her mother's absence, Janie pondered the situation. She was grateful for her parent's assistance, yet wished she could do without it, because she felt she was approaching Lance Winter in an underhand manner. Instead of facing him boldly, she was creeping towards him from behind his aunt's skirts, and with Janie this went against the grain. But what else could she do?

Restlessly, she carried the coffee mugs to the kitchen, where she washed and put them away; then, returning to the sunny veranda, she listened to the low murmur of her mother's voice. A glance at her watch told her the conversation had already lasted ten minutes, and she could only sit in one of the basket chairs while curbing her impatience as she awaited the outcome.

When Laura returned to the veranda, her eyes held a gleam of satisfaction. 'Well, it's all fixed,' she smiled. 'Nell expects to see you late this afternoon.'

'What did you say to her?' Janie asked apprehensively. 'You *did* tell her about the interview, I hope?'

'Of course. And I explained that you'd been given— what did you call it? Oh yes, the brush-off. She immediately made excuses for him. She declared he's so busy—and so *worried*.'

'Oh? Why should he be worried?'

'Apparently the shearing gang is due to arrive— although they could be held up because of rain—and he insists upon being in the shed during that period.'

Janie nodded. 'That's not surprising. Daddy always maintained the boss should be on deck during the shearing. But why should it *worry* him?'

'His worry is mainly the polo ponies. The shepherd who exercises them has broken his arm. It's a compound fracture, which will keep him from work for several weeks, and that also means he'll be unable to work with the ponies.' Laura sent Janie a significant glance as she added, 'Nell said for you to be sure and bring your jodhpurs.'

Janie's jaw sagged slightly. 'My—my joddies?'

'Of course. Don't you *see*? The moment Nell told me about the poor man and his broken arm, I saw you taking his place. Naturally, I reminded her about how you used to spend hours in exercising your father's ponies, and it was she who said to be sure to bring your jodhpurs. So, there you are—it's all settled.'

'But my *real* reason for being there—what was said about *that*?'

Laura brushed the question aside with an airy gesture. 'Oh, well, we talked about it and decided to just let matters ride.' She chuckled. 'That's good, isn't it? Let matters *ride*——'

'What do you mean?' Janie felt apprehensive.

'We agreed that Nell wouldn't mention the interview to Lance. We thought it better to let events take their course.'

'Won't he wonder why I've suddenly arrived from out of the clouds?'

'Nell will tell him you're the daughter of an old friend, and that she's invited you to stay for a few days. That's the truth, isn't it?'

'Maybe it *is* the truth, but I don't like it.' Janie stood up and began a restless pacing about the lounge until she swung round to face her mother. 'This is an underhand approach. I feel it's dishonest.'

'Nonsense. You're exaggerating the situation.'

'The moment he hears my name he'll be suspicious.'

'I doubt it. Personally, I think he'll be so thankful to see his polo ponies being exercised, he won't be able to think of anything else. Few men can see further than their noses.'

'Oh, yes?' Janie still felt doubtful. 'Something tells me you might be underrating this particular man.'

Laura gave a small shrug. 'It's possible, dear. However, I've done my bit. There's your opportunity. Take it or leave it.'

'I'll take it. Thank you for arranging it, Mother. I'd better get myself ready.' She swung round and left the room.

It was late afternoon when Janie reached the Golden Hills property. As she drew near the coast, the land became hilly, causing the rises and falls of the road to become acute, until a glimpse of the blue Pacific stretching towards a distant horizon indicated she had almost reached her destination.

And, suddenly, there it was: an entrance flanked by concrete pillars, one of which bore the name of the place in stainless steel letters. Beyond it, the drive curved round the contour of the hill until it reached a flat area where the two-storeyed homestead nestled within the shelter of evergreen macrocarpas, pines and gums.

Bordering the circular lawn which lay between the house and the shelterbelt, a spectacular curve of flowering cherry trees caught her eye. Some lifted high branches laden with deep pink blooms, while others stretched in more horizontal growth, their limbs bowed with pale, hanging clusters. Yellow forsythia and brilliant azaleas grew beneath them, but all this could be examined later, Janie decided, as she skirted the lawn to stop near the front entrance.

As she did so, the door opened and she had no difficulty in recognising the petite woman who came down the steps to greet her. At the same time she noticed that Nell Abbott's hair had more silver streaks than she remembered, and she also imagined her face to be more lined. However, it was the same bright, friendly voice that welcomed her.

'Janie, how lovely to see you after all this time? It seems ages since your mother and I watched the matches. We enjoyed them so much, even if there were anxious moments, but I'm afraid those days have gone. She lost her man and I've lost mine.' She sighed, then appeared to pull herself together as she changed the subject. 'Now, then—let me look at you.' The grey eyes scanned Janie's face. 'My goodness—you're an attractive girl! That hair is so golden—those eyes are like bluebells.'

Janie laughed. 'Thank you, but I'm afraid you're flattering me.' She'd been told often enough that she was easy to look at, but she never gave it a second thought.

Nell then observed the small suitcase being lifted from the car. 'You don't appear to have brought much luggage,' she said with a hint of disappointment. 'I was hoping you'd stay for at least two weeks or more.'

Janie stared at her in amazement. 'A *fortnight*?'

'Yes. Well, come in and meet Lance and Maud. You'll remember Maud, of course. She's still with me, thank goodness.' Then, pausing to lay a hand on Janie's arm, she whispered, 'By the way, when Lance came in for lunch I told him I'd invited the daughter of an old friend to stay for a few days. I didn't tell him *why* you were coming. He's very touchy about reporters, so just take it *slowly*.'

Janie recalled the abrupt manner she'd encountered on the phone. 'Has he a reason for this attitude?'

'My dear, it's because he feels they don't always write about things as they really are. Some reporters twist the truth for the sake of sensation, but I'm sure you're not in that category——'

'Otherwise you wouldn't have invited me here. I want you to know I'm very grateful,' Janie assured her.

Nell smiled at her, 'I'll be honest. When your mother rang, I couldn't resist offering the invitation. I liked your parents very much, and somehow I felt that to have you here would be like reviving those happy times. I suppose I'm a silly old woman.'

'Old? Mother says *old* is a swear word, Mrs Abbott.'

'Lance would agree with her. He doesn't like to hear me call myself old. He's inclined to call me little Nell—and I'd prefer you to call me Nell rather than Mrs Abbott, if you don't mind.'

Janie placed an impulsive kiss on her cheek. 'Little Nell is sweet and it suits you.' Privately, she was surprised because the endearing term did not fit in with her preconceived idea of Lance Winter. In her opinion, even his own name was against him. It was cold and bleak.

She followed Nell up the steps and into a wide hall which had several doors opening from it. A staircase rose on their left, and beyond it a door opened into a living-room occupied by two people.

'Here she is!' Nell exclaimed happily.

Maud came forward with a smile of welcome. 'We're so glad you could come,' she said with sincerity.

She was just as Janie remembered her, tall, grey-haired, well-rounded and bearing an air of capability. But while she returned Maud's greeting she was vitally conscious of the man who had risen to his feet. She had tried to avoid looking at him, but with Nell's introduction her eyes were drawn towards him as though dragged by an invisible magnet and, as her gaze became locked by his, Nell's voice floated over her head.

'This is my nephew, Lance Winter—and this is Janine Meredith.'

He was an outdoor man, dark-haired, above average height and of athletic build. The silver-grey of his hand-knitted jersey was stretched across broad shoulders and chest, while dark green cavalry twill trousers fitted snugly to slim hips.

He broke the silence, his voice deep as he murmured.

'Janine Meredith—I've heard that name somewhere.'

Nell spoke quickly. 'Of course—at lunch time when I told you Janie would be arriving this afternoon.'

'Perhaps. Yet I feel I've heard it before today.' His eyes narrowed thoughtfully as he continued to regard her.

Maud spoke to Janie. 'We were just having a cup of tea. I'm sure you could do with one after that long drive. Milk and sugar?'

She was grateful for the diversion, and as she took the tea from Maud she hoped it would help quell the mad fluttering going on within her breast. Of course he'd heard her name before today. He'd heard it on the phone—but with a bit of luck it might not have registered sufficiently to enable him to remember. At least, not yet.

She became aware that his eyes continued to regard her intently. They were unusual eyes she noticed, trying to decide on their colour. They were neither brown nor grey, but perhaps a dark hazel. It was difficult to ignore them— or him, for that matter—and there was that definite sensuousness about his finely chiselled mouth. She jerked her thoughts into some sort of control.

'Janine Meredith,' Lance said again, his voice still little more than a soft undertone, as though pondering the question.

It told Janie there was lingering doubt in his mind. It had the effect of making her feel like a hypnotised rabbit, crouching in the long grass from the searching eyes of a hawk.

Nell turned towards him, almost with a touch of impatience. 'Haven't you heard me speak of the Merediths? Janie's father and your uncle played in the same team. Laura and I always watched the matches together. It was when you were in the South Island, but I've spoken of them.'

'And Janie is also keen on polo?' A smile played about his lips as he turned to her.

Apprehension rose within her. Oh, heavens, here it comes—this is where he remembers, she thought with a sense of panic. But before she could do more than nod, Nell had found an answer.

'We really didn't see much of Janie, because she always seemed to be taking care of her father's horses.'

His eyes lit with sudden interest. 'You're used to handling horses?'

'I lived with them until Father died,' she explained. 'He had four polo ponies and I helped with their training.'

'You *did*?' His interest deepened.

Nell sent him a significant look. 'I suggested that Janie should bring her jodhpurs. I thought that perhaps she wouldn't mind giving you a hand—now that poor Peter Bryant's been put out of action.'

A grin betrayed his pleased surprise. 'Nell, you're a beauty. Of course she could be a godsend.' He turned to Janie with a hint of enthusiasm. 'How long can you stay?'

'I—I haven't any real ties,' she admitted, feeling a hypocrite.

'Good. I hope you'll settle in. To be honest, I couldn't understand why Nell had invited you here. There's so little going on in this out-of-the-way place, and no company for a girl, apart from two dear souls who spin wool every free moment.' He paused to send Nell a hard stare. 'Actually, I was a little suspicious of her motives, but now I can see she had help for me in mind.'

Maud spoke sharply. 'Why should you be suspicious of Nell's motives? You know perfectly well that your interests come first and foremost with her.'

'Yes, that's just the point,' he drawled back at Maud. 'The burning question lies in which direction those interests were heading.'

'I don't know what you mean,' Maud returned calmly.

'No?' He sent her a mocking smile.

The meaning of their exchange was lost upon Janie,

although she sensed that each was handing the other an underlying message. And while looking more closely at Maud she realised that here was a dominant personality upon whom Nell probably leaned. It would be Maud who really ran this house, she decided.

Lance's deep voice interrupted her musings. 'Do you intend to drink your tea standing up, or would you be good enough to sit beside me on this window seat?'

She obeyed meekly, and as she sat with her back to the last of the sun slanting rays shone through her hair to form a golden halo. Unaware of it, she wondered why he stared so intently, and a slow flush crept into her cheeks as his close examination included her clear complexion, the deep blue of her eyes and finally came to rest on the curve of her lips. Embarrassed, she turned away and was in time to catch a significant glance flick from Nell to Maud.

Lance spoke at last. 'So you've handled horses. At what age did you learn to ride?'

'I was four when Santa Claus brought my first pony. It was a dear little grey.'

'And you say you've handled polo ponies?'

'It was mainly their exercising as the season approached.'

Maud cut in drily, 'One would imagine you were interviewing Janie for a job.'

Lance grinned at her. 'OK, Maud—I'm now willing to concede that it was in the sporting field where Nell had my interests at heart. She realised I was in a fix.'

Janie looked at him wonderingly. 'What other inter-ests——?' She stopped suddenly, then apologised. 'I'm, sorry, that's no concern of mine. I shouldn't have asked that question.'

'Forget it,' Lance said abruptly. He peered into her empty cup. 'If you've finished your tea, I'll show you the ponies.' He stood up, took her cup and saucer, and carried them to the table.

Maud uttered a protest. 'Give her a chance to have a second cup.'

'The horses will be waiting near the stable yard,' he said briefly. 'It's time for their evening feed.' His dark hazel eyes swept over Janie. 'Of course, if you'd rather sit and drink more tea——'

She stook up hastily. 'No, thank you. I'd prefer to come out to see the horses.'

The living-room door opened on to the back veranda, and, leading her through it, he took her down steps and along a path bordered by the brilliant heads of polyanthus. They crossed the drive, and the path then continued towards a small gate leading into a paddock.

He pointed out tractor and implement sheds, and while she tried to concentrate on these details, the fact that she was walking so closely beside him on the narrow path made her feel almost light-headed. However, sanity returned as they reached a dark red stable with hayloft. It was situated beside a yard, enclosed by white rails, and beyond the yard four horses waited patiently.

'Perhaps I can help you,' she said eagerly.

He ran appraising eyes over her suit. 'Not in that attractive outfit. You might collect dry mud from one of the night rugs. For the moment, you'll be allowed to say hello to each member of the team.'

The remark surprised her. She hadn't expected him to notice what she was wearing, and she could almost hear her mother say, 'I told you so,' as her mind flipped back to the advice she'd been given.

'What shall you wear, dear?' Laura had asked. 'I'd advise that nice yellow, brown and white tartan kilt and waistcoat with your white polo-neck jersey. The days aren't yet too warm for it. And you must take your new jade check to change into for dinner. It's dressy, without being overdone.'

Janie had laughed. 'OK, Mother! You've arranged the

visit, you might as well complete the job by arranging the wardrobe.'

'I'm only trying to help, dear. It's always important to make a good first impression,' Laura had reminded her daughter.

'Good impression? Upon whom, Mother?'

'Upon Lance Winter, of course,' Laura had declared flatly.

Janie had sighed with exasperation. 'Mother, you're so transparent! I know I'm twenty-three, but I do not yet consider myself to be on the matrimonial shelf. I couldn't care less about making a good impression upon this—this fellow who was so rude to me on the phone. If it weren't for the story I want, I'd gladly punch him in the eye.'

'You might feel differently when you meet him,' Laura had pointed out slyly.

Janie had given a sniff of derision. 'That's most unlikely! You're forgetting that my opinion of him is already well established, and I can tell you right now that he's a long way from being my ideal man.'

And now it seemed as if her own words were being flung back in her face. Mother had been right in thinking she'd feel differently when she met him. Watching, she liked the way he spoke to the horses as though they were his friends, and when he sent an unexpected smile towards herself she could only wonder why her legs felt so weak.

CHAPTER TWO

LANCE opened the gate on the far side of the yard. The horses entered and walked sedately to where four railed stalls were equipped with covered feed boxes.

'They always go to the same stall,' he told Janie, removing a halter from its hook beside a feed box, and placing it over the head of a dark bay gelding. 'Come and meet Major. He's the senior of the team. Last year, several players wanted to buy him, but he knows jolly well I wouldn't part with him.'

'How does he know?' Janie asked, smiling as she stroked the smooth coat.

'Because he knows I'm always pleased with him. He's so darned good out on the playing field. When the game's over he tosses his head as if mighty satisfied with himself, but if I'm not riding him he stands pawing the ground with impatience. I always take two to a match,' he added, rubbing the white blaze on the dark nose.

Janie said, 'Daddy always took two or three ponies to a match.' She blinked rapidly, breathing deeply to control the overwhelming memories.

Lance moved to the next horse which was a grey. 'This is Dandy. He, too, has had his three years of training, and I've also had offers from players who'd like to buy him, but one doesn't part with a good friend. I'm afraid I'd never make a horse dealer,' he added with a wry grin.

Janie nodded. 'I know how you feel. It's easy to become fond of an animal, but difficult to let it go. There's also an old saying about a good horse never being sold.' This man had feeling for his horses, she realised, and despite her preconceived ideas she found herself in sympathy with him. This did not mean he was having an effect on her, she assured herself firmly. It was merely an understanding from one who had also suffered the experience of having to part with beloved animals.

'The next two are fillies,' Lance explained as he put halters on first one and then the other. 'This light bay is Joy, and the chestnut is Gay.'

'Gay is beautiful,' Janie said, running her eyes over the filly's perfect proportions.

'You can start with her in the morning, if you like. At least—that's if the decision is made for you to give me a hand.'

'Decision? Whose mind has to be made up—yours or mine?' she asked lightly.

'My own mind is not yet settled on the question,' he admitted.

She turned surprised eyes upon him. 'I thought you needed help.'

'That's all too obvious—but to be honest I'm not too sure of the situation, or your own intentions. It seems to be just too much of a coincidence for a horse-riding angel to flap her wings in my face at this precise moment. Excuse me, I'll fetch their feed.'

He strode towards the table before she could answer, and the satirical ring of his words was not lost upon her. What did he mean by her *intentions*? Was he suspicious of her motive for being there, and did this mean that her identity had now clicked in his mind?

Watching him disappear into the gloom of the wide-open door, she came to a decision of her own. Yes, she would stay and give him assistance, not because of the story she wanted, but because the familiar atmosphere of those dear departed days of her old life now had her in a firm grip.

As for the magazine article, she'd forget it. She'd write to the editor and say, 'Sorry, it's quite impossible.' No doubt he'd cut the tie that held her as a stringer, but this was something that couldn't be helped. Nor was his the only magazine in the country, she thought with a sense of relief.

She became aware that Lance was leaving the stable with a bucket of food in each hand. She pushed her recent deliberations aside, gathered her wits amd moved to lift the lids from the feed boxes, while he poured a mixture of crushed oats and chaff into each one. The ponies began munching at once, the railings between them preventing any fast, greedy eaters from stretching over to rob a neighbour.

Night rugs were then brought from the shed, and as Lance buckled their straps Janie's previous fears returned to her. She told herself that she was now in a situation where her integrity was at stake. Lance had only to discover the real reason for her presence and he'd consider her to be dishonest. The thought made her cringe. It was something she'd be unable to bear.

It meant there was only one course for her to take. At the first opportunity, she would tell Nell of her intention to scrap her plans to prize a story out of Lance. No doubt he'd consider her to be a person who threw in the towel easily, but that couldn't be helped.

Lance buckled the last strap, then straightened his back. 'Some are slower eaters,' he said. 'We'll leave them to finish at their leisure. In the meantime, I'll show you the way to the beach.'

Leaving the yard, he led her behind the stable, then along a metal road that ran beyond a shelterbelt of ancient pines. Large cones lay on the ground, and when she accidentally trod on one she would have overbalanced but for his hand on her arm. She gave a shaky laugh, while uttering a word of gratitude, and as she turned to look at him she was surprised to catch a strangely inscrutable expression in his eyes. It vanished in a flash and she then wondered if it had been her imagination.

Releasing her arm abruptly, he brushed the incident aside as he said, 'Have you ever ridden horses on the sand or in the sea?'

'Yes. They like the feel of it, but I know one has to be careful.'

'Sometimes I bring the ponies down to the beach. They love the sea when they get to know it, and they're very fond of swimming.' He paused, then asked, 'Why do you say one has to be careful?'

She sent him a look of amazement. 'Because if you let them go in too deep, they're capable of heading out to sea. Surely you're aware of that?'

'Of course I know it. I merely wondered if *you* knew it.'

She felt a sudden irritation. 'In other words, you were testing me. You were wondering just how stupid I could possibly be.'

'Apart from the fact that they're valuable polo ponies, I'd hate to think of you and Joy or Gay being washed up on the coast of Chile.'

She ignored the slur of her intelligence. 'I suppose not everyone realises that horses will start swimming out to sea and go on and on.'

He made no reply and they walked in silence until they reached a gate in the shore boundary fence. The road then became little more than a firm track that led down to the beach. It was bordered by high tufts of coastal-growing marram grass, and as they came to the firm sand they paused to look at freshly made hoof-marks.

Janie noticed their small size. 'These prints have been made by a pony—perhaps a Shetland,' she guessed.

'Observant girl,' he approved. 'They'll be Tinker's prints. Young Sam will have been on the beach.'

'Who is Sam?'

'He's the eight-year-old grandson of the Strangs, who own the neighbouring coastal property.'

She looked back to follow the direction of the hoof-marks. 'They seem to come from the boundary gate. Would he have visited your house?'

His tone became casual. 'Who knows? Actually, he's Penelope's boy. She's the daughter of the Strangs. You'll meet her, if you're around for long enough.'

'That'll be nice,' she remarked with forced brightness, wondering why there was a niggling doubt at the back of her mind.

Lance said, 'Penelope had a spot of bad luck in the matrimonial field. She's divorced and has come home.'

'Oh?' It was difficult to keep the ring of curiosity from her voice, nor did she miss the sympathy that tinged his own tones. Eventually she asked, 'What happened to cause the break-up?'

'I've no idea. She hasn't been home for longer than six months, and I don't ask questions. Possibly it's what's known as "other woman trouble".'

She smiled. 'I see. You're taking her side without knowing all the facts?'

'I know Penelope. We went to school together—at least, until boarding-school days.'

'And of course you went to dances together?' Why did she want to know these details? His denial came as a surprise.

'Not really. When she left school she travelled overseas, and by the time she returned I was working in the South Island. Now that I think of it, we really haven't seen a heck of a lot of each other—until recently.'

'Ah, but you're seeing a great deal of her now—therefore you automatically believe her to be in the right,' Janie said softly. Then, before she could control her tongue, 'You must be very fond of her.'

He sent her a side-long glance. 'Is it unusual to have a soft spot for somebody one has known since childhood?'

'I suppose not.' And then impulse made her ask, 'Has Nell also a soft spot for Penelope?'

He gave a short, mirthless laugh. 'If she has, she keeps it well hidden. Neither Nell nor Maud appear to be on her side. For some obscure reason, they refuse to give her the benefit of the doubt.'

'But *you're* sure the fault in this situation lies with the husband. How can you be so positive?'

'I'm not positive,' he retorted testily. 'And please don't suggest I'm setting myself up as a judge. One must know every detail of a situation before one is capable of judging the rights or wrongs of a case.'

'I'd have thought Nell would have seen it in that light.'

He took a deep breath that was almost a sigh of weariness. 'I suspect the trouble really lies with Maud. She's a strong-minded woman with set opinions about right or wrong. Nell places great store upon what Maud declares to be black or white.'

'Is she always right?'

'You can usually bet on it—at least nine times out of ten. But I mustn't criticise her. She's been a tower of strength to Nell, and I can't imagine how I'd cope with my aunt if Maud left.'

'Anyone can see they're fond of each other.'

'It was Maud who taught Nell to spin. It's an activity that's given her an interesting hobby, and I'm grateful to Maud for it.'

Janie's eyes flicked to his broad shoulders and chest. 'I can see your nice jersey is homespun and hand-knitted.'

'Maud's work.' He grinned briefly. 'You're allowed to feel its softness——.'

'I'll take your word for it,' she retorted coolly.

Their steps had taken them along the stretch of beach where the sand was damp and firm. Gulls wheeled overhead, and Janie was about to stoop for a shell when the sound of a child's voice floated on the breeze. 'Hi, Uncle Lance!'

They turned to see a boy riding his Shetland pony towards them.

'Hi, Sam,' Lance responded.

'You're related?' Janie asked, surprised.

'No, it's merely a courtesy title, insisted upon by his mother.' Then, to the boy, 'You can say hello to Miss Meredith, Sam.'

Sam's brown eyes surveyed her from beneath straight black hair that fell across his brows. 'Hi,' he muttered briefly, then turned to Lance again. 'Mum sent me with a message, but I couldn't find you. She sent me to tell you she's home again.'

Lance scowled. 'Did she, indeed? Where has she been this time?'

'Auckland, I think,' Sam said vaguely. 'She bought lots of new dresses and—and a new game for me. She said to tell you to come soon.'

'OK—message delivered,' he muttered gruffly. 'Thank you.'

Janie giggled as she sent Lance a teasing glance. 'Shall you rush off at once—or have your evening meal first? I'll let the horses loose for you.'

Sam sent her a penetrating stare. 'Are you a visitor?'

Janie nodded. 'I suppose you could say so.'

'Can you ride?' the boy demanded.

'Of course she can ride,' Lance cut in. 'Janie will be helping with the polo ponies until shearing is over.'

'What'll she be doing?' Sam wanted to know.

'She'll be exercising them.' Lance explained patiently. 'The time has come for them to be put into training, because the polo seasons begins in December, They can't go out on to the field unless their muscles have been built up.'

'Huh. Girls can't ride. I bet she falls off.' Sam's scornful tone held unconcealed belligerence.

Janie was startled by the boy's antagonism, which seemed to indicate that he'd taken a dislike to her. Could it have arisen on behalf of Penelope? Was it possible that, even at his tender age, he objected to the sight of Lance in the company of someone other than his mother? Ridiculous! She was being over-imaginative.

Forcing herself to smile at him in a friendly manner, she said, 'This is a nice pony. What's his name?'

'Tinker.'

'I hope that doesn't mean he gets up to tricks.'

'Tinker's OK,' he said with a hint of sulkiness.

Determined to keep her tone amicable, she said, 'I can see you ride well. You must know the rules.'

He looked puzzled. 'What rules? I don't know any rules. I just get on and Tinker goes.'

'There are rules for good riding,' she assured him. 'There are lines you must learn. Your head and your heart keep up—your hands and your heels keep down; your legs are close to your horse's sides and your elbows close to your own.'

The boy looked at Lance for confirmation. 'Is that right, Uncle Lance? Does *she* know——?'

Lance nodded. 'Repeat them twice and you'll remember them.'

Sam did so obediently, then looked at Janie with a flash of new interest, before cantering away towards a gap in the sandhills.

As they watched him disappear, a smile touched her lips, and then a light laugh escaped her. 'Don't tell me—let me guess. He's your *go-between*,' she accused teasingly.

He swung round to face her, his eyes narrowed in anger.

'What the devil do you mean?'

'He's the message boy, of course. Why did Penelope use him rather than the phone? Is she afraid of getting short shrift from Maud, who could possibly answer it?'

'Certainly not!' he snapped. 'Maud might imagine she rules the roost, but she knows her place and exactly how far she can go.'

'Perhaps Penelope's afraid the message might not be passed on.'

'Nonsense,' he gritted with suppressed anger, as he swung round and began to retrace her steps. 'It's time we were getting back,' he flung over his shoulder.

She was forced to run to keep up with the long strides that took him over the sands—nor did it need his silence to tell her he was thoroughly irritated. She cursed her unruly tongue, for she was now well aware that she had no wish to be at loggerheads with him, and knew also that his manner of communication with Penelope was not her business.

However, his anger appeared to have evaporated by the time they reached the ponies, which were waiting patiently in their stalls. He examined the feed boxes to make sure each animal had eaten its full ration, and then he turned them loose into the field.

The daylight was fading when they returned to the house, and as they entered the living-room Nell sent Janie an aplogetic smile. 'My dear, I should have shown you your room when you first arrived. You don't even know where you'll be sleeping. Lance will carry your suitcase upstairs——'

But Lance had left the room, and Janie said hastily, 'Please don't worry, I can carry it. It's very light.' It had been left in the hall near the front door, her camera and small cassette tape recorder with its built-in speaker resting beside it.

Nell led her up the stairs to the upper hallway. At the

top, she paused to say, 'There are five bedrooms along this passage, four of them opening out to the balcony. The one on the left is my room and next to it is Maud's room. Then comes Lance's room, and I'll put you next to him in the end single room. The fifth bedroom and two bathrooms are across the passsage.'

She ushered Janie into an attractive room, decorated in deep rose and white, and she pushed back the long floral drapes to open the balcony door.

Janie walked through to gaze at the view. Through the dusk she could see the stable, and beyond the trees lay a glimmer of white surf breaking on the beach.

'Get yourself settled, then come downstairs,' Nell advised. 'I think dinner is almost ready, and Lance always insists upon having a drink before we sit down.'

'I'll not be long,' Janie promised as Nell left the room.

She placed her camera and cassette recorder on the dressing-table, then opened her case to hang her dresses in the wardrobe. She laid her jodhpurs and blue jersey over a chair in readiness for the morning, and then went to freshen up in the bathroom.

When she returned, the sound of a muted, whistled tune indicated that Lance was in his room.

He sounds happy, she thought. *Of course*—Penelope had come home. He would be going to visit her. Strangely, the certainty of it caused a sudden cloud to hover above Janie's head, and there seemed to be little she could do to brush it away.

Staring at her reflection in the mirror, she told herself it was pointless to take pains over her appearance—at least on *his* account—because, with his mind on Penelope, he wouldn't even notice she was there. Nevertheless, a few quick strokes with a comb set her golden hair in place, while a smoothing of colour emphasised the generous curve of her soft lips.

When she went downstairs, she paused in the hall to peep into the spacious lounge with its comfortable good quality furniture. A dining-room adjoined it through a wide archway, each room opening on to the veranda. They appeared to be rooms for formal occasions, and when she went into the living-room she was struck by its homely atmosphere and the comfort of its open-living design.

It was really a combination room, because one end of the long area was taken up by kitchen facilities, divided from the main room by a tiled bench set above cupboards. Bookshelves lined one of the walls, and in the far corners two spinning wheels stood beside baskets of wool. Pine logs blazed in the open fireplace, dispelling the chill of the evening air, and the table was set with place mats, resting between sterling silver cutlery.

When Lance came downstairs, Janie noticed he'd changed into blue trousers and a bone-coloured jacket and shirt. The light shades contrasted with his dark hair and tanned complexion, making him look even more handsome than before. No doubt Penelope would approve, she thought with an inward twist that only served to darken the cloud still hanging above her head.

Nell also noticed his change of clothing. She watched him pour pre-dinner sherries and then, her eyes full of reproach, she said, 'Surely you're not—going out?'

'Correct guess, Nell.' He did not elucidate, nor did his tone invite further questions.

'Well, really, I thought you could have stayed home this evening,' Nell said in an aggrieved voice.

'You did? May I ask why?' he demanded mockingly.

Janie turned to Nell quickly. 'Please don't think he has to stay home on my account. I'm sure that wherever he's going must be most important.' She peeped at him knowingly, as he handed her a finely cut crystal glass.

He sent her a cool glare, then took up her unspoken

challenge. 'If you must know, I'm going to see Penelope,' he told them.

Nell's mouth tightened visibly, while Maud's brows became raised as she stared into her glass. Neither said a word.

He went on affably, 'Pen's just returned from Auckland.'

'*Laden*, no doubt,' Maud remarked acidly.

'If she's brought you a present, I'll bring it home,' he promised, grinning at the remoteness of this possibility.

Dinner was a fairly strained affair, with everyone chatting valiantly to combat the tense atmosphere. Nell obviously disapproved of the fact that Lance was going to visit Penelope, and while Janie told herself she couldn't care less, she was, at heart, disappointed.

A short time after the meal, she met him in the front hall. He appeared to be ready to leave the house, therefore she said quickly, 'You haven't told me what time you'd like me to start in the morning.'

He looked at her thoughtfully. 'Be out at the stable yards by eight o'clock. I want to see you ride—to make sure you've got hands before you really get to work.'

She was startled by the suggestion, her eyes widening as she looked at him with indignation. '*Hands?*' she exclaimed.

'Yes. It's that little something you're born with—if you're lucky. You can call it an instinctive sympathy a good rider is able to establish between himself and his horse.'

'I *know* what you mean by *hands*,' she retorted coldly. '*Some* people are born with it—others might or might not acquire it.'

His mouth twisted ironically. 'In that case, I'm sure you'll understand that I don't want the sensitive mouths of my ponies ruined by rough handling.'

Janie's chin rose as her fury mounted. 'They'll not find any unnecessary force coming through my hands,' she snapped at him in cold tones. 'However, if you doubt my ability to handle them in a decent manner, why don't you arrange for Penelope to do the job?'

'Unfortunately, Pen's not a good rider,' he admitted reluctantly. 'In fact, she dislikes horses—otherwise she could have been doing the job ages ago.'

'Perhaps she's afraid of them,' Janie pointed out. 'Very well, I'll see you out at the yard at eight. You'll be able to judge whether or not my hands are good enough for your precious polo ponies.' Irritation still simmered within her. *Of course* she had hands. It was something that had often drawn her father's praise.

He nodded briefly, then informed her in cool tones, 'Don't worry, I'll know at once. In the meantime, you'd better put your car in here.'

She looked at him blankly. 'In here?'

'That's right.' He turned on a switch, then opened a door set below the stairs.

Peering beyond him, Janie saw that it led into a three-door garage she'd noticed set a short distance past the front entrance. It housed a silver-grey Volvo and a blue Austin Mini.

Lance rolled up the two end doors. 'This garage was added long after the house was built,' he told her. 'Put your car in the space beside Maud's Mini.'

'Does Nell drive?' she asked, wondering if his aunt possessed a car.

'No. She becomes nervous in traffic, but Maud surges through, and other vehicles give way very smartly.'

'Are you saying she's a reckless driver?'

'Determined is a better word. But she loves to drive, and by giving Maud the Mini I felt Nell would be assured of transport to wherever she wishes to go.'

She watched him get into the Volvo, and as the car swept round the curve of the drive she became even more conscious of her own disappointment. Although she tried to brush it away, she knew it had been caused by his departure and the knowledge that he wasn't even remotely interested in becoming more closely acquainted with her.

She sighed as she watched the flash of carlights disappear beyond the trees across the lawn. As far as he was concerned, the important matter of the moment was to rush to Penelope. She'd sent the message and he was away like a rocket. So what did *she* care? *Not one iota!*

She stood still until darkness engulfed the drive beyond the shelterbelt, then fetched her car keys to put the Subaru in the garage. When she returned to the living-room, she found Nell and Maud still busy in the kitchen area. The automatic dishwasher was rumbling its way through its load, and while Maud finished wiping the benches Nell turned apologetic eyes towards Janie.

'My dear, I'm so sorry Lance has seen fit to go out on your first night with us. It's really very naughty of him.'

Janie's smile was disarming. 'Does it matter?'

'Of course it matters,' Nell said firmly, her voice echoing barely concealed irritation. 'I'm hoping you'll get to know each other really well, and you can't do that if he's gadding off to see Penelope every evening.'

'Does he go to see her *every* night?' Janie queried mildly, while making an effort to appear little more than vaguely interested.

'Too often for my liking,' Nell retorted with an edge to her voice. 'I can't help feeling worried about it.'

'Perhaps she has a—a strong call upon him,' Janie suggested.

Maud uttered a derisive sniff. 'More like a stranglehold,' she declared darkly.

Janie kept her voice light. 'I can't imagine anyone having a stranglehold on Lance Winter—unless he's a willing victim,' she added as an afterthought.

Maud turned to face her. 'Of course you're right—but is he the victim of the mother or of the boy?'

Janie could only look at her in puzzled silence.

'What do you mean, Maud?' Nell asked querulously.

Maud wiped her large, capable hands, then led the way to the living-room area. As they sat down, she said, 'I believe Lance is sorry for the boy.'

Janie felt doubtful. 'Are you saying that Lance goes to see Penelope because he's sorry for her *son*?'

Maud smiled. 'I'm saying that Penelope is making ground with Lance *through* her son.' She nodded, her mind obviously well settled about her summing up of the situation.

Nell shook her head vaguely. 'I'm afraid your meaning is—is out of my reach.'

Maud sighed with infinite patience. 'Well, look at it this way,' she went on, as though explaining the matter to a child. 'I think much of the trouble lies in Lance's pity for the boy. He knows the lad has lost his father, and no doubt he recalls the time when he lost his own father.'

Nell frowned dubiously. 'Yes, well——'

'Try to imagine that little boy's life before his parents were divorced,' Maud pursued. 'There would be constant quarelling and bickering between them—trouble enough to send the poor child into a state of nervous insecurity and misery. Then would come the traumatic experience of parting from his father. And what does he find when he reached his grandparents' home? Nothing less than a nice man living nearby—a man who is kind and doesn't quarrel with his mother.'

'A man who has *horses*,' Nell chimed in. 'Sam is mad about horses. Yes, I see what you mean.'

'For the first time in years, the boy is happy,' Maud concluded.

Janie sent Maud a penetrating glance. 'Sam calls Lance

"Uncle", but in his own mind he's really adopted him as his father. Is that what you're saying, Maud?'

'I'm convinced of it,' Maud declared. 'I dare say that most of his schoolmates have fathers, so you can be sure that Sam also wants to lay claim to one. And you can be sure that his mother is shrewd enough to take advantage of the situation. As it is, the lad comes and goes on the property as he wishes—and you mark my words—before long his mother will be doing the same.'

Nell gave a cry of protest. 'Stop it, Maud! You're making me feel quite frightened.'

'Don't say you haven't been warned,' Maud muttered firmly. She pulled her spinning-wheel away from the corner and began to treadle as she fed a handful of soft, fluffy, carded grey wool into the eye of the spindle.

It was a sign for Nell to follow suit, and as Janie watched both wheels turning to the rhythmic treading she felt compelled to ask timidly, 'Am I right in assuming you wouldn't like to see Lance marry Penelope?'

'Indeed you are.' Maud's tone was firm.

Nell's foot movement paused and the wheel became still while she moved the spun yarn to the next hook on the flyer. Answering Janie's question, she explained, 'My dear, it's not that there's anything *wrong* with Penelope—it's just that we feel she's not *right* for Lance.'

Janie said, 'I see.' Actually, she did not see at all. Didn't these two dear souls realise that it was Lance who had to decide who was right or wrong for himself—and that his wife had to be someone of his own choice? She thought about these facts for a few moments, before curiosity forced her to say, '*Why* isn't Penelope right for him?'

Nell paused again, this time to lift a handful of soft wool from the basket beside her. 'It's not easy to say these things,' she said in a low voice, 'but you must understand that I've known Pen since she was a small child. I've watched her

grow up, and I know she has always been a selfish
demander who does nothing for anyone, unless she herself is
to benefit in some way. I would prefer to see Lance married
to someone who is a little more willing to give.'

'There's more to it than that,' Maud added. 'If Lance
brings her in as mistress of this house I'm afraid Nell and I
will find difficulty in remaining here.'

Janie shook her head doubtfully. 'I can't imagine Lance
wanting you to leave. Besides, Penelope would need your
help in running this large house.'

Maud's mouth tightened. 'Perhaps—but don't you see?
It would be a matter of incompatibility. Neither Nell nor I
would have any wish to stay here with Penelope lording it
over us both as mistress of the house.' She turned to the
small woman. 'Isn't that so, dear?'

Nell gave a deep sigh. 'Yes, I'm afraid it is—but that's not
the *point*. I want to see him married to someone who will
make him *happy*, and I don't believe Penelope has the ability
to do that.' She sent Janie a faint smile. 'I suppose you think
I'm a silly old woman for worrying over a man of his age.
He's thirty-two now, but you must remember he's the only
"son" I've ever had.'

'She wants the best for him,' Maud said, stating the
obvious, 'and to be honest—so do I.'

To be honest. Maud's last words jolted Janie's memory
towards the admission she must make to Nell. She sat in
silence, watching the turning wheels and the spun yarn
filling the bobbins, until at last she said, 'Speaking of
honesty—I've decided against trying to get an interview
out of Lance.'

Nell was mildly surprised. 'Oh? Why is that? You can
speak openly, because I've told Maud about it.'

'Oh, yes—I know why you're *really* here,' Maud smiled.

Janie felt embarrassed by her own change of mind. 'I
might as well admit that the thought of doing it niggles at

me. It makes me feel I'm here under false pretences, and I hate the dishonesty of it.'

'So you'll allow the opportunity to slip through your fingers?' Nell asked in a quiet voice.

'Yes, I suppose so.'

'Does that mean you intend to go home?' Maud's query held sharp anxiety, as she stopped treadling to stare at Janie.

'No. I've promised to help with the ponies, and I'll do what I can until I'm no longer needed.'

'Lance will be grateful!' Nell exclaimed.

'I'm really being selfish,' Janie admitted with a further burst of honesty. 'I love riding, and it'll be a pleasure to be handling horses again, especially polo ponies. You can call it nostalgia, if you like.'

Later, as she lay in her bed, she admitted the truth of this fact. The nostalgia had begun from the moment of taking her jodhpurs from the cupboard at home, when she had tried them on to make sure they still fitted her. They had been worn only a few times since that ghastly day when her father had been rushed from the polo field by ambulance, and now, as she turned to look at them, showing clearly in a shaft of moonlight, her thoughts also turned to Topsy, her black mare.

Since her father's death, the Riverslea property had been leased, but arrangements had been made for Topsy to remain on the farm. Janie paid grazing fees for her, and had permission to ride her whenever she wished, but the occasions had been few, because the heartbreak of losing her father was still too strong to make cantering along the riverbank a pleasure.

Even on her way to Golden Hills she had stepped on the gas when approaching the turn-off to her old home. Tears had blurred her vision, until she had shaken herself mentally and had told herself she should be grateful that

Riverslea had been leased rather than sold, and that she was able to keep Topsy on its lush pastures.

Several miles further south, a signpost had indicated the route to the coast, and as she'd reduced speed for the left-hand turn she had taken a deep breath. Riverslea and the mountain ranges were now behind her, while ahead lay the fresh fields owned by the man who had been so antagonistic on the phone.

Thinking of him, she moved restlessly in the bed. What was he doing at this moment? What was the situation between him and the woman they called Penelope? Was he in love with her—as Nell and Maud seemed to fear? And why hadn't he married her before she'd gone away to marry somebody else? There must be answers to these questions, she thought drowsily, as her eyes closed.

CHAPTER THREE

WHEN Janie woke next morning, the sun was still casting a glittering path to dapple the sea from the eastern horizon. Bright pink clouds floated against the blue of the sky, and as she gazed at the vivid, gold-edged colours, the old saying sprang into her mind: red sky in the morning, shepherd's warning. It meant that rain was not far away, and that shearing would be further delayed.

She dressed hurriedly, stepping into her jodhpurs and pulling the deep blue jersey over her head. A matching zipper-front jacket was taken from the wardrobe, and she went downstairs.

Maud was already in the kitchen. She cast an admiring glance over Janie's slim form and said, 'Jodhpurs suit you. And that jersey makes your eyes look like—like——' She fell silent, lost for words.

'Like old-fashioned blue bags that have been given a swirl in the wash and then stuck on my face!' Janie laughed. 'That's what my father said when he gave me this jersey and jacket to wear when exercising his ponies.'

'And now wearing them takes you back to those days.' Maud guessed, her eyes holding a shrewd glint.

Janie nodded without speaking. It was all too true, but now was not the moment to begin discussing those days. Tears were apt to rise too readily, and she had no wish to face Lance with red rims round her eyes.

She ate the cereal and poached egg on toast that Maud placed before her, then ran lightly along the path towards the old red stable. The horses were already in the white-railed yard, their night covers removed, and Lance was busily grooming Major, the dark bay gelding.

He paused, dandy-brush in hand, to stare at her across Major's withers. 'Good morning, Blue-eyes,' he said at last.

She sent him a brief smile. 'Good morning. If you've a rough brush, I'll remove the mud from Gay's legs.'

He nodded towards the left. 'It's over there on the rail.'

She expected him to continue with Major's grooming, but his eyes remained upon her, taking in every detail of her appearance. She knew they rested upon her face and neck before moving to the rounded swelling beneath her blue jersey, and, as she watched their descent to her jodhpur-clad hips and legs, a deep flush began to stain her cheeks. It was almost as if he had mentally undressed her, and the thought made her feel uneasy.

At the same time, she became acutely aware of an intangible magnetism that not only emphasised his masculinity, but seemed to draw her towards him. She resisted its force, telling herself she was not a simpering schoolgirl about to swoon at his feet. While it was an effort to drag her eyes from the handsome face, she turned to where the brush lay on the rail.

He watched her work for several moments before he said, 'I can see you've done that job before today.'

'You can say that again,' she retorted, her eyes misting slightly, as everything her father had taught her flooded back into her memory.

A gentle but constant murmur escaped her lips, soothing the filly as she brushed the way the hairs grew. As she leaned against the hind quarter to attend to the tail, she knew that observing glances were flashed in her direction.

Later, when the dandy-brush had completed the grooming of each horse, Lance said, 'Do you think you could ride Gay and lead Joy?'

'Of course,'

'In that case, we'll saddle up and I'll show you the

exercising route. I presume you know that ponies being prepared for playing need to be walked and slowly trotted up and down hills for at least two hours daily?'

'That's to build their muscles,' she informed him sweetly. Did he imagine her to be entirely ignorant about these matters? Then, as her gaze swept over the surrounding contour of land, she added, 'At least you have the hills for the job.'

'Peter and I usually give them two hours in the morning and another in the afternoon, part of it being pole work. You know what I mean by pole work?' He sent her a sidelong glance as they walked towards the stable to collect saddles and bridles.

'I've done pole work, if that's what you're asking,' she told him drily, adding by way of assurance, 'The poles are set upright at short intervals and the ponies are ridden in and out between them in a zigzag manner. They are really an aid to practise turning and changing feet——'

A sudden silence fell upon her as they entered the stable, with its bins for oats and chaff, its saddle racks, each with a peg beneath it to hold a bridle. There were shelves holding grooming equipment, buckets and large stable brooms, the entire scene bringing her to a halt, while she breathed in familiar smells. At the end of the shed, a steep stairway led up the hayloft.

Lance followed her gaze towards it. 'That's where Peter Bryant fell,' he said.

'You mean the man who has broken his arm? How did it happen?'

'I can only assume it was sheer carelessness. He was cleaning out some of the winter hay when he stepped backwards on to the stairs, and down he went before he could clutch at the railing. At least, that's the story I've been given, but I suspect there's more to it.'

'The poor man——' Her voice held genuine sympathy.

'If he'd stepped off the landing at the front opening, he might have broken his neck instead of his arm. Lord only knows how long he'll be off work,' he added gloomily.

She could understand his frustration. 'No doubt it leaves you short-handed—but haven't you anyone to take Peter's place? Aren't there other men working on the farm?'

'There are two others, but they're not keen on horses. In any case, they prefer to use farm motorbikes.'

'Aren't some of your hills too steep for bikes?'

'Yes. Sid and Don are then forced to use horses, and that's when I've observed their handling of them. It made me put Peter in charge of the polo ponies.'

'I can understand that his accident causes him to be a real loss.'

He nodded, frowning. 'At the same time, I must keep things in proportion, and I don't want to take Sid and Don from other important work that has to be done. There's general maintenance, such as repairs to the boundary fence, to say nothing of constantly going round the sheep, which are apt to become cast when in full wool.'

She said, 'I know about sheep becoming cast. I've dragged many sheep back on to their feet—but aren't the shearers due soon?'

'The gang will arrive when the weather permits them to complete other sheds in the district, but in the meantime rain has delayed their progress. Sheep have to be dry for shearing.'

'I know.'

He ignored this further reminder that she had been brought up on a farm by explaining, 'Against all the work that must be done, the ponies are merely a sideline. They constitute my *sport*, and I can't allow them to take precedence over the running of the property. It would be most irresponsible.'

'Well, in the mean time, you've got me,' she consoled.

He spun round to face her. 'Thank heavens for you!' The statement came fervently, as he stepped closer to her.

She looked up into his face. 'Providing I've got *hands*, of course,' she reminded him quietly.

He took her hands in his, turning them over to examine the palms. 'Something tells me they'll be more than capable,' he murmured as, unexpectedly, his hands dropped hers to grip her shoulders. He stared down into her face, his eyes holding a strange light as they swept her features.

He's going to kiss me, she thought wildly. How dare he imagine he has the right to do so? But as his head bent swiftly, hardly aware of her actions, she raised her face to meet the firm mouth that came down upon her own.

She told herself it was meant to be no more than a casual, brotherly kiss, indicating gratitude for the fact that she was there and willing to help. Nevertheless, it stirred an excited tingling somewhere below the region of her throat, causing a sensation which jerked her pulses into action. As his lips left her own, she was forced to catch her breath.

The grip on her shoulders loosened abruptly, while he almost pushed her away from him. He said nothing as he turned to lift a nearby saddle from its rack, then snatch at the bridle, to sling it across his shoulder.

The action reminded her of the horses waiting outside, and as he strode from the stable she pulled the neighbouring saddle from its rack and followed him back to the yard, where everything seemed normal. In fact, it was all *so* normal that it was as though the kiss had never happened, and for several moments she wondered if it had been her imagination.

But her quickened heartbeats told her that this was not so, and again she assured herself it had been merely a brief exposure of his inner relief—a tangible display of thankfulness that the ponies would be exercised by someone who knew what to do. Not that she'd yet proved this fact to him, but she felt confident her ability would soon be observed.

Within a short time she had the saddle and bridle on Gay, and a leading rein on Joy. Her riding helmet was snatched up from where she'd dropped it earlier, and as she fastened the chinstrap she saw that Lance was already leaving the yard.

He rode Major while leading Dandy, and as he made his way along the farm track he turned to watch the manner in which she handled the two fillies. There was a brief nod of approval as she approached. 'Joy's not the first horse you've led,' was all he said.

A small sigh escaped her. 'Those days are part of another life.'

'Tell me about them.' The words came almost as an abrupt command.

The request surprised her. Was he really interested—or did he feel obliged to make polite conversation? Whatever his reason, she needed little encouragement to talk about Riverslea, and soon found herself launched into what was almost a saga of other days.

It was like pouring out her soul to someone who could understand all that had been lost, and she knew he listened attentively. He was unlike the city friends she'd made—the people who did not realise that farming was a totally different way of life.

There were times when he interrupted to ask a question, but before very long he'd heard about her work as a landgirl and the training of the polo ponies, all of which led up to her father's death, the leasing of the property and the move to Napier.

'You were never bored?' he asked. 'So many girls find that country life is not sufficient for them.'

She gave a light laugh. 'Father always feared the day

would come when I'd long for the city lights. To guard against it, he encouraged me to take up a hobby—something to give me an extra interest.'

'Your mother had a hobby?'

'Yes. She's another spinner. The wheel kept her happy for hours, and this made him determined that I should have my own special recreation—something quite away from farm work, and something needing mental stimulation.'

'Oh? What sort of hobby did he have in mind?'

'He reminded me that literature had been my best subject at school, and he persuaded me to take a course in short story writing——' She stopped suddenly, appalled by her own unguarded words. What on earth had got into her? She must be out of her wits to begin babbling about the very thing she intended to keep hidden.

He was politely interested. 'You were successful?'

'Oh, I—I scribbled a bit. I dabbled in it a little until the upheaval of my father's death threw everything out of gear.'

'Did you ever reach the stage of having a story published?' There was quiet persistence behind the question.

'A few stories eventually saw the light of day.' The admission came reluctantly, before she added with forced gaiety, 'That's enough chatter about me—I've done nothing but talk about myself. Now it's your turn. Tell me how Golden Hills got its name. At the moment, they're so very green it should be Emerald Hills—so why Golden?'

'Because they were golden when my great-grandmother first set eyes on them. Soon after my great-grandfather had bought the land he had some of the hills ploughed and then sown with rape to be used as food for the sheep. However, there was a delay in getting the stock to the place, and before any had arrived the rape had matured and burst into flower. My great-grandmother stood gazing at the masses of golden blooms covering the hills and declared there was only one name for the property.'

Janie's eyes became misty as a flight of fancy took her mind back into the past. 'I can almost see her stepping down from the buggy,' she mused. 'I feel sure she'd be a tall, slim woman with dark hair. She'd be wearing a hat tied on with a veil, and perhaps a cape over her long, dark skirt.'

His swift glance betrayed surprise. 'Did Nell show you a photo, or is that your writer's imagination coming to light?'

Hastily she shied away from a return to the subject of her literary efforts by pointing to a distant slope of gently rising ground. 'Wouldn't that be a suitable place for trotting uphill?'

'That, as it happens, is our destination, but first we'll call at the woolshed to check the number of woolpacks we have in hand. We don't want to run short of sacks to carry the shorn wool in the middle of shearing.'

They rode without speaking, the only sounds in their ears being the plod of the horses' hoofs on the soft turf, or the occasional bleat of a sheep. Lance led the way, crossing the field to the right until they came to a metal farm road, and as they followed it round the curve of a hill a large timber building came into view.

Painted dark red, with white facings, it was surrounded by numerous yards divided by white rails. Four low openings along one side told Janie it was a shed where four shearers would stand in a row while manipulating the electricity-powered handpieces that would remove the wool from each sheep.

Woolly animals, grazing near the shed, scattered as they approached. A dog gave raucous barks of welcome, its noise being enough to bring a man to the wide sliding-door entrance. He paused on the landing, then came down the steps to cross the yard to where they waited at the outer railings.

'Hi, boss,' he grinned cheerily, his eyes sweeping Janie with undisguised interest.

Lance introduced them briefly. 'Sid Brown—Miss Meredith.'

She was then dismissed from the conversation while they discussed the number of woolpacks on hand, the radio weather report, the present whereabouts of the shearing gang and its progress through the neighbouring flocks to be shorn.

Eventually Sid said, 'Any news of Peter Bryant and the state of his arm? I've heard rumours that it's worse than we feared.'

Lance nodded gloomily. 'Yes, I'm afraid that's right. He won't be handling horses for a while, or anything else for that matter.'

'A while meaning what——?'

'A couple of months at least, or perhaps longer. Who can tell?'

Sid's eyes turned to Janie. They were full of appraisal. 'In the mean time, you appear to have found assistance.'

'I'm fortunate in having an aunt who knew where to turn,' Lance admitted gravely.

Janie glanced at him quickly. Was there a puzzled gleam in his eye? Was he wondering how his aunt had been able to pluck assistance from out of the blue?

Sid continued to regard her. 'She sits that filly very nicely. Looks as though she's part of the animal. Not like that other—um—I mean—not like your neighbouring friend.'

'If you're referring to Penelope Russell, why don't you say so?' Lance's voice had an edge to it. He reined Major round and with Dandy in tow began to leave the rail.

Sid sent Janie a grin that was accompanied by a sly wink. 'Stick to him, girlie,' he muttered in an almost inaudible voice. 'Stick to him good and hard——'

She felt faintly indignant. 'I—I beg your pardon?'

'I think you heard what I said.'

'I don't know what you mean.'

'Don't you?' He grinned again. 'Well, naturally, I mean that you should keep up the good work with those ponies.'

'Oh, I'll do that all right,' she flung over her shoulder, as pressure on the rein and lead rope caused Gay and Joy to follow Lance.

Sid Brown's remarks had puzzled her. For one silly moment she'd thought he'd meant something entirely different, but of course *that* would be ridiculous. He'd meant to stick to *them*, meaning the *horses*—not to *him*, meaning *Lance*.

The metal road, which had been constructed to take heavy trucks to and from the woolshed, now continued towards an open-sided Dutch haybarn, and as they made their way towards it Janie saw the poles set at intervals over a flat stretch of ground.

'I've wondered when I'd see poles,' she said, then, as she began to count the eight uprights, splashes of rain hit her face. '"Red sky in the morning, shepherd's warning,"' she quoted. 'Did you see it?'

'Do you mean that brilliant sunrise? Yes, I saw it, and now there's a shower coming. We'll take shelter in the haybarn.'

They dismounted beneath the high roof that protected the last few bales of winter hay. Lengths of baling twine lying on the ground enabled him to tether the horses to the barn uprights, and as he did so they lowered their heads to nibble at tasty wisps lying within reach.

A black cat emerged from the warmth of a broken bale, stepping forward with feline grace to rub itself against Lance's leg. He swept it up into his arms. 'This is Cinders,' he informed Janie as his well-shaped hand stroked the soft fur. 'She lives in this haybarn and attends to all mice who decide to take up residence.'

Janie had a strong liking for cats, and as the green eyes turned to stare at her, she said, 'She seems very friendly—please let me hold her.' Then, as Cinders was transferred into her arms, loud purrs issued from the furry throat. 'There, now—she *likes* me.' The words echoed satisfaction as she fondled the animal. 'Cats don't usually like strangers.'

'Anyone would like you, Janie,' Lance said quietly.

The remark surprised her and, looking up, she found him watching her with an intense expression in his eyes. Returning his gaze, she tried to fathom its meaning, and even as she did so it vanished. She bent her head again, wondering if it had been her imagination, yet knowing that this had not been the case.

Then he took Cinders from her arms. The cat was placed on the ground, and as his hands went to her shoulders suspicion surged that he was about to kiss her again. A slight trembling of indecision took possession of her mind while she tried to tell herself what she should do about his—his utter *temerity* thinking he could kiss her whenever he wished. And yet, once again, there was something that urged her to lift her face towards his.

But instead of kissing her he searched her eyes as he demanded in quiet tones. 'Have you had a row with your boyfriend?'

The question startled her. 'What makes you think so?'

'The fact that you're here, of course.'

A light laugh escaped her. 'Do you always jump to conclusions in this manner?' Disappointed, she lowered her chin to its normal level.

'Girls of your age don't run away without reason.'

'*Run away?* You must be raving!'

'Am I?' He paused, frowning. 'Come on—be honest. Who have you left at home?'

'Only my mother,' she smiled, telling him the truth,

because she had no particular boyfriend.

Unconvinced, he said, 'Don't dodge the issue. Who is he—and why did you quarrel?'

'Why do you want to know?' she hedged, puzzled by his interest.

His frown deepened. 'That's something I've been asking myself, especially as I know it's not my business. I can only imagine it's all tied up with the miracle of your arrival— someone capable of working these ponies.'

She regarded him seriously. 'Isn't Nell's explanation sufficient? She knew you were in a difficult situation, and she also knew of my existence——' She fell silent, the falseness of her own statement almost choking her. She had *not* come primarily to exercise his ponies. She had come to interview *him*, and even if she had now decided against this latter course she felt she was living a lie. In her own mind she was a hypocrite, and the knowledge was bitter.

She also knew that sooner or later she would have to admit the truth, but instinct warned that now was not the moment. If she so much as muttered the words 'interview for a sports magazine', she feared she'd be thrown out on her ear. And she was enjoying the taste of her old life too much to allow that to happen. Oh, no—it would be much wiser to wait for the right moment.

His voice cut into her ponderings. 'You still haven't told me what it was all about.'

She looked at him blankly. 'What was what about?'

'The upset with the boyfriend.'

Exasperated, she snapped, 'Please understand that I haven't a serious boyfriend. Nobody rushes to my door as you apparently rush to Penelope's——' She stopped suddenly, appalled by her own words.

His eyes narrowed. 'Ah. You've been listening to little Nell—with Maud putting in a few well chosen words.'

'Not at all——'

'Be honest—they've been having their say in the matter of Penelope and myself.'

'Surely you can understand they have your interests at heart?'

'Yes, of course I'm aware of that fact.' His eyes scanned her face. 'It's why I wondered if you'd been brought here for a purpose.'

'A—a purpose?'

'To be laid across my path, as it were——'

Her eyes widened in disbelief as a slow flush crept into her face. 'Are you suggesting that Nell invited me here in a—a deliberate attempt to—to break your romance with Penelope?'

'I wouldn't put it past that same small person.'

'Then you *are* having a romance with Penelope?' His eyes had become accusing.

'I didn't say that,' he snapped.

'But you don't deny it,' she challenged, a shaky laugh escaping her. 'Personally, I don't believe that Nell would bring me here for such a reason.'

'Wouldn't she? Nell's a deep one. Don't forget that she looks upon me as her son. Something tells me that if I marry Penelope she'll be most upset.'

'Then—you have considered doing so?' She made the question sound casual, then waited breathlessly for his answer.

The broad shoulders lifted in a nonchalant shrug. 'There have been moments when I've wondered about it—and there have been other moments when I've thrust the thought aside. Moments like these, for instance——' His arms enfolded her, drawing her closer to him in a firm embrace.

Her pulses leapt as she went unprotestingly, leaning against him as though she had no power to resist the warmth of his clasp. Nor did she have any wish to do so.

His head bent slowly, causing her to hold her breath, and the blood quickened through her veins as his firm mouth sought her own. Her lips parted to the deepening of his kiss, and as she responded to the ardour of it she heard the drumming of the rain on the haybarn roof. Or was it the hammering of her own heartbeats?

His strong fingers seemed to burn through her jacket and into her flesh as they kneaded the muscles of her back, creeping down her spine towards her hips. She knew that his masculinity had been aroused and was calling loudly to be satisfied. The demand was enough to bring her to her senses, and a small gasp escaped her as she pushed against his chest.

'Shouldn't you be remembering—Penelope?' she panted.

There was a dazed look in his eyes. 'Penelope? Who's she?'

'You know very well who she is——'

'Oh, *Penelope*—I really wasn't thinking of her at the moment.'

'But—shouldn't you be?'

'I'm not engaged to Penelope—despite Nell's fears.'

Again his arms drew her close to him, pressing her against his lean length in a manner which was completely possessive. He gazed deeply into her eyes, his head bent slowly and his lips had almost reached her own when the unexpected sound of a motorbike reached their ears. He froze, his arms dropping to his sides as he stepped away from her.

Moments later the bike, ridden by a young man, came into view. His oilskin coat shone as the rain fell upon it, and as the popping noise of the motor ceased his sharp blue eyes took in the scene of the man, the girl and the horses sheltering in the haybarn.

Lance greeted him nonchalantly. 'Hi, Don—this is Miss Janine Meredith.' He paused as he regarded the freckled face beneath the oilskin hood. 'Has some special reason brought you to the barn?'

Don's eyes dragged themselves from Janie. 'It sure has, boss. It's the small matter of a little something for Cindycat.' He took a bottle of milk from a bag attached to the back of the bike, then went in search of Cinders' empty bowl.

They watched as he lifted Cinders for a brief petting before filling the bowl. He then returned to the bike, and as he flung a leg over the seat he swept them with swift glance. 'I'm afraid the rain is just about over, boss,' he remarked in a dry tone. There was a roar from the revving motor and he was away, slithering precariously in places.

Janie peeped at Lance. Had he caught the implications of the man's remark? Would he now continue from where Don's arrival had forced him to leave off? It seemed unlikely, because he was now peering up at the sky, and she became aware of a sense of anticlimax. Or was it—disappointment?

When they left the haybarn the sun was shining again, the air smelled fresh and sweet, the fields looked as though they had been newly washed. Janie turned Gay towards the long gradual slope she'd noticed earlier, then became aware that Lance was heading in a different direction.

'We'll go to the poles,' he called over his shoulder. 'I'd like to see how you handle them.'

She sent him a wry smile. 'I don't blame you for making sure I know what to do. If I can't put them between the poles, I might as well give up all idea of exercising them.'

He made no reply, until they reached the line of uprights where he said, 'I'll hold Joy while you put Gay through.'

She knew she was about to be put to the test, but she felt confident of her ability as she passed him the rein of the filly she'd been leading. She then set off to circle in a loosening-up canter before entering the line of poles. They stood at about eight feet in height, their purpose being to serve as a practise area for the rapid turning which became necessary during games of polo.

The poles were not new to Janie, and as she approached them she reined to a sedate trot. Zigzagging between them, she used the pressure of knees, leaning and rein to turn Gay, and on reaching the end she trotted back. The second time along the line was made at a canter, and when she returned Lance nodded approval.

'I can see you're an old hand at the poles,' was all he said.

'My father had his line,' she responded. 'During the practice season it was part of my day's work.' She sighed deeply, thankful for the knowledge her father had imparted, and knowing that without it she would not be riding in the company of this man, to whom she felt so strangely drawn.

They spent almost an hour at the poles. Saddles were changed, and the four horses were given, in turn, a period of zigzagging between the uprights. Janie was in her element, and by the end of the period she felt as if she'd never been away from the task of exercising polo ponies.

Dandy was the last to be put through, and when the grey gelding had finished his run they made their way towards the long slope where they put in a further period of slow trotting up and down hill.

Eventually Lance said, 'That's enough for this morning. During the afternoon, they can be walked for about an hour or more.'

'Perhaps on the beach,' she suggested.

'A good idea,' he agreed. 'They like the sands.'

They rode in silence for a short distance while thoughts appeared to occupy his mind. He didn't even turn to look at her when he said, 'You've not yet told me you'll take on the job.'

She stared straight ahead. 'I don't recall a definite

request being made.'

'How long can you stay?' The question came abruptly.

Impulse almost made her tell him she could stay for as long as he needed her, but instinct warned her to ask casually, 'How long would you like me to stay?'

'Until Peter Bryant returns—and heaven alone knows when that will be.'

She recalled the small suitcase she'd brought. 'I'd have to go home for more clothes.' It was difficult to keep the eagerness from her voice.

'I'll drive you to Westshore. Nell and Maud can come with us for the outing. They enjoy going to Napier for a day's shopping.'

'Mother will be delighted to see Nell,' Janie assured him. 'They haven't seen each other for ages. I'll phone and tell her we're coming,' She rode in silence, until a thought made her turn to look at him doubtfully. 'Are you sure you can spare the time? I can easily take them in my car. And what about the horses?'

'They can have a rest for the day.' In the pause that followed his words, the only sound to be heard was the gentle thudding of the horses' hoofs on the turf, but at last he continued, 'While you're at Westshore, I'll visit my accountant. There are a few matters to be discussed, one of them being yourself. You'll be put on the farm payroll.'

Her eyes widened as dismay echoed in her voice. 'Oh, no! I don't need wages for doing something that'll give me so much pleasure.'

'You're forgetting my side of the deal. I don't take charity,' he informed her coldly. 'I'll see if I can make an appointment for this coming Friday.'

'I'll ring Mother and tell her to expect us for lunch,' Janie said, being well aware of Laura's capabilities and her love of entertaining friends.

'You'll do nothing of the sort,' he snapped. 'You're

mistaken if you think we'll land on her for lunch. You'll ring and tell her to be ready by noon, and instead we'll take her to lunch.'

'Oh——'

'We'll go to that restuarant overlooking the sea and then you can spend the afternoon at Westshore while I visit my accountant.'

'Are you always so fiercely independent?'

'It's possible.' The reply came tersely.

After that they rode without speaking, and the unbroken silence gave Janie the opportunity to wonder what there was about this man that gave her an unaccustomed sense of inner excitement. Apart from his handsome features and obvious virility, was it his command over most situations?

The subject of the proposed trip to Napier and Westshore was almost forgotten until later, when Lance mentioned it during lunch.

Nell beamed with pleasure. 'That'll be lovely, dear—and so nice to see Laura again. We'll take her shopping with us. Only this morning Maud said it's time we took a run to Napier to search for new knitting patterns.' She paused as doubt clouded her grey eyes. 'But when do you intend to go?'

'On Friday—if it can be arranged.'

Nell beamed again. 'That'll suit us nicely, dear. Tomorrow is the gardener's day and on Thursday we have Country Women's Institute.'

'Did you think I'd forgotten those small details, Nell?'

'I must say, you seem to remember most things,' Nell admitted.

Maud put in a sly remark. 'So you won't have forgotten that you are expecting a visitor this afternoon.'

A surprised glance was shot across the table. 'I am? It's news to me. Who is this visitor I'm supposed to be expecting, Maud?'

Her brows rose. 'Surely you haven't forgotten that Penelope is coming?'

He frowned. 'Penelope? Are you sure? How do you know about this visit, Maud?'

'Because she phoned this morning.' She looked at him with unconcealed interest. 'Don't tell me you've *forgotten*? But perhaps you've been so very busy with the horses—and with *Janie*, of course——' Maud's smile became broad. 'Naturally, all thoughts of this afternoon's arrangement have gone out of your head.'

But Lance saw no humour in the situation. He sent Maud a direct stare. 'Tell me—what, exactly, did Penelope say?'

'Not very much, apart from the fact that she'd recently returned from Auckland and that she'd brought a present for Nell. It's a silk scarf.' Maud looked at him curiously. 'Are you sure she didn't mention it last night?'

He shook his head. 'I don't think so.'

Maud said, 'I asked her why she hadn't given it to you last night, but she said she preferred to give it to Nell personally. She also said that she told you she'd come here this afternoon to do so. *Now* do you remember?'

Still frowning, he shook his head. 'My memory must be slipping,' was all he said.

CHAPTER FOUR

NELL looked round the table in a slightly bewildered manner. 'I'm sure it's most kind of Penelope to bring me a present from Auckland, although I must say I'm amazed.'

'Just accept it gracefully,' Maud advised.

Nell changed the subject by turning to Lance. 'How did the morning ride go? Did you take Janie to the poles?'

He nodded, then said with satisfaction, 'Yes, she took the ponies through with ease. I watched her leaning and using her knees like an old hand at the game.'

Nell sighed happily. 'I'm so pleased. And this afternoon——?'

'We'll take the ponies down to the beach. The tide should be well out.'

Janie turned to him quickly. 'There's no need for you to come if you're expecting Penelope. I can manage the ponies—I'll take first one pair and then the other——'

His jaw tightened. 'I am *not* expecting Penelope. There were no arrangements made for her to come this afternoon. We shall go to the beach and walk the horses along the edge of the water for at least an hour—and if she's still here when we return I'll say hello to her then.'

Nell said, 'It's possible she'd like to meet Janie. I presume you told her that Janie will be staying with us for a while?' The question came innocently.

'Yes, I might have mentioned her,' Lance admitted casually.

Janie caught the rapid glance that slid from Maud to Nell; and, although she waited, neither said anything further on the subject of Penelope. At least, both managed to avoid her name until lunch was over and Lance had disappeared outside. Then, as Janie helped to clear away the dishes, Maud became eloquent.

'I really believe Lance is right,' she declared. 'There were no arrangements made last night. Penelope is coming here this afternoon for the sole purpose of casting her eyes over Janie. She fears a potential rival,' she added with mounting conviction.

'Do you think so?' Nell's voice held suppressed excitement.

'I'm sure of it. Nor do I believe she bought you a present in Auckland. The scarf is merely an excuse. She's always going off to some place, and never once has she brought home a gift for you—so why start now?'

'Better late than never,' Janie suggested on Penelope's behalf.

Maud shook her head. 'I don't want to disappoint you, Nell dear, but I'll bet this scarf is one of her own—hardly used and now ironed and wrapped in tissue paper, unless she had wrapping paper handy. And there will lie the test. If it was bought recently, as a gift, the wrapping paper will be new, shiny and uncreased.'

Nell laughed at Maud's deductions. 'You're a dreadful woman, and full of suspicions!' she protested.

'Give Penelope the benefit of the doubt,' Janie pleaded. 'I can't see that she has anything to fear from me.'

'Can't you?' Maud's tone was dry. 'Well, at least Nell will get a new silk scarf out of it.'

Nell shook her head, but said nothing. However, the worried frown on her usually smooth brow seemed to indicate she had no wish to accept a gift from Penelope.

Janie left them to go in search of Lance. She found him at the stable, and a short time later the four polo ponies were being taken towards the beach. Janie rode Dandy and led Joy, while Lance, mounted on Major, led Gay.

Nothing was said as they walked towards the gap in the pine plantation. The sound of hoofs on the metal farm road was like music in her ears, and, half closing her eyes, she tried to imagine she was back at her old home. But it was impossible to do so because her awareness of the man riding beside her was so strong it swept everything else from her mind.

When they came to the shore boundary gate, Lance leaned down to open it, throwing a remark over his shoulder as he did so. 'You'll need to become used to riding each of the four ponies.'

'I'll look forward to having a good gallop on Major,' she responded, casting admiring eyes over the dark bay gelding.

'I'll tell him to behave himself,' Lance grinned, closing the gate after Joy had been led through it.

'Doesn't he always behave himself?'

'He can become stroppy. There are times when he needs a strong hand. Yours appear to be rather small to contain much strength.'

'I can be determined,' she defended.

'Can you, Janie? In all matters?' He turned to look at her.

Meeting his gaze, she had the sudden feeling that he now referred to something totally different from the handling of horses. Nor did she consider it wise to probe for further explanation.

The tide was low when they reached the beach. The sand was firm and they made their way across it towards the water's edge. As they splashed through the ripples, Lance said, 'The salt water is good for their fetlocks, and walking on the sand makes them work their feet in a manner which strengthens their pasterns. But I suppose you know all that.'

She nodded cheerfully, while the fresh sea breeze blew colour into her face. She felt a glow of exhilaration, its cause, she told herself, lying in the horses and having nothing to do with the fact that was she riding beside Lance Winter.

'You're smiling,' he said unexpectedly. 'Is something amusing you?'

She shook her head. 'No, it's just that I feel so happy. It's probably written all over my face.'

He turned to stare at her. 'May I ask—what's making you happy?'

'I suppose it's the fact that I'm doing what I love doing best of all. I'm out riding. I'm having a wonderful day.'

It was true. And coupled with the pleasant day on horseback was the fact that she'd been kissed by this—this devastating man, who was capable of stirring the heart of any girl. Was he in the habit of kissing every girl he met? The thought was a disturbing one, although—what could it matter to her?

Her thoughts seemed to reach him, causing him to ask, 'Is it a day that will live in your memory?'

'Oh, yes! Most of it will stay with me for a long time—although parts of it will eventually be forgotten,' she forced herself to add lightly.

They spent an hour walking the horses along the water's edge, and during the latter part of it Janie noticed Lance glance at his watch on more than one occasion. He's got Penelope on his mind, she thought, with a sense of disappointment.

At last he said, 'It's time we were going home.'

'Yes, of course, she'll be there by now.' Her voice reflected her despondency.

He sent her a sharp glance. 'She? Oh, you mean Penelope?'

'Of course—who else?' Her tone was still dismal.

'Yes, I suppose she'll be there,' he agreed.

'Then we must hurry,' she said, in a tone casual enough

to disguise her reluctance. For some strange reason, she had no desire to meet Penelope.

But he said, 'Hurry? There's no need for haste. We're supposed to be walking the horses—remember?'

His words gave her spirits a lift, and she told herself she was being a fool to allow the thought of Penelope to worry her—even before she'd set eyes on the woman. But they sank again as, drawing near to the stable, her attention was caught by the sight of a yellow car parked in the yard at the back of the house.

'Your visitor has arrived,' she remarked with a forced smile. 'I'll put the saddles away while you go to her.'

'Don't be silly,' he retorted. 'We'll do the job together and we'll go to meet her together.'

She looked at him curiously, then asked, 'Do I detect emphasis on that word *together*? Are you trying to tell her something?'

'It's possible. It's time she—well—never mind about that.' He dismounted, and began to remove the saddle from Major's back.

Janie looked at him thoughtfully. What had he been about to say? Did he intend to show Penelope she wasn't the only shell on his own personal beach? But, as she removed Dandy's saddle, she brushed the notion aside as being ridiculous. However, as they carried the saddles to the stable, she became conscious of an underlying apprehension, and she knew she had no wish to meet Penelope.

The feeling remained with her as they went towards the house, and although she tried to brush it away she was assailed by the suspicion of being observed from one of the windows. This was proved to be a fact when a tall, slim woman came through the living-room door, crossed the veranda and walked along the path to meet them. Even before they drew near to each other, Janie could see that she was beautiful, and that she appeared to be endowed with a cool elegance, which was emphasised by the smart red dress with its black spots and wide black belt.

Penelope's black hair was arranged in a smooth, sophisticated style, and her eyes glittered from behind slightly narrowed lids as they surveyed Janie's closely fitting jodhpurs, her slim waist and the rise of rounded breasts beneath her blue jersey.

Lance's introduction was brief. 'Penelope Russell—Janine Meredith. I understand you're the bearer of a gift,' he added, grinning as though the thought amused him.

'Yes. I told you about it last night. Have you forgotten I said I'd bought a scarf for Nell and that I'd bring it to her this afternoon? The words were addressed to Lance, yet the dark eyes remained upon Janie.

Lance frowned at her in disbelief, then shook his head. 'I have no recollection of it. I must be getting senile.'

Penelope laughed. 'Oh, well, it's easy enough to forget one small detail when we've so much to talk about—and to plan.'

The dark brows rose. 'We plan——?'

'Of course we do. When we're alone, we just seem to go on and on about so many things that are of mutual interest. And *you* know the things that interest us *both*.' She smiled knowingly into his face as she took his arm in a possessive manner.

They continued to walk towards the house but, as the path was not wide enough to take three abreast, Janie was forced to fall in behind. She was given the feeling of being deliberately ignored by Penelope and suddenly discarded by Lance, and it became necessary to crush an impulse to brush past them and race ahead towards the homestead.

This action, she realised, would make her look stupid and childish, therefore she had no option but to remain behind to observe Penelope's careful, model-like walk, and her attitude towards Lance. The dark-haired woman's modulated voice was kept to a low pitch, perhaps because what she said was for Lance's ears alone, and Janie noticed there were times when it was necessary for him to bend his head to hear what was said. It enabled Penelope to brush his ear with her lips, nor did she fail to grasp at each opportunity to do so.

When they reached the house, Maud was pouring tea into cups of fine bone china set on an embroidered cloth laid on the living-room table. There were plates containing home-baked fruit cake, iced sponge cookies and fingers of Scotch shortbread, all of which indicated that Maud's cake tins were seldom empty.

Also on the table was a silk scarf in colours of vivid yellow, lime-green and black. It lay unwrapped on a piece of crumpled tissue paper and, as Janie looked across it towards Maud, the latter's eyes seemed to say, I told you so—tissue paper—and those aren't Nell's colours——

Lance also looked at the scarf. He picked it up, fingering its texture as he said to Nell, 'Very cheerful. It'll be a change from all your blues, pinks and mauves.'

'It's time she got away from those old pastel shades,' Penelope declared firmly. 'Brighter colours will give her a lift.'

'I'm sure it's very kind of you,' Nell said nervously.

'I'd like to take you in hand,' Penelope said with decision. 'I *hate* blue. I'd get you out of it like a shot.' She swept a contemptuous glance over Janie's jersey.

'Which is your favourite colour, may I ask?' Maud drawled in dry tones.

'Why—red, of course!' Penelope retorted without hesitation. 'It's the colour of magic.'

'*Magic?* What rubbish!' Maud's tone had become slightly scathing, then she turned to Janie. 'Do you believe that red is the colour of magic?'

Janie laughed. She had no wish to openly disagree with

Penelope, therefore she compromised by saying, 'It's said that fairies, elves and the Little People in Ireland wear red caps. Don't you remember the old poem? "Up the airy mountain, down the rushy glen, we daren't go a-hunting for fear of little men; wee folk, good folk trooping all together, green jacket, red cap and white owl's feather."'

Lance said, 'I'd better find myself a red cap.'

'You're aiming to work some magic?' Penelope asked lightly.

'Something like that,' he admitted evasively.

'Perhaps we can work it together,' she suggested eagerly, an unspoken message shining unguardedly from her dark eyes.

Nell gave a discreet cough, then changed the subject. 'Tell me, Penelope—how is young Sam doing at school?'

'Very well, I believe,' Penelope said with pride. 'You know, he really does love Lance,'

'Is that a fact?' Nell's mouth tightened.

Janie made an effort to become included in the conversation. 'We met him down on the beach. He was riding Tinker.'

Penelope ignored her, by turning to Lance. 'I've been meaning to talk to you about that Shetland pony,' she said. 'In a short time, Sam will be too heavy for it. Father knows of a fourteen-hand pony that's for sale. It's supposed to be foolproof. He's sure it would be suitable for Sam, but I refuse to buy it without your approval. It's coming home on trial on Friday, so I'll expect you in the afternoon.' She looked at him expectantly.

Lance shook his head. 'Not on Friday. I'll be taking Janie to Westshore. Nell and Maud will be with us.'

Penelope's eyes widened with sudden interest, as she turned to Janie, smiling at her for the first time. 'Oh, so you're going home so soon? Well, I suppose it's been a pleasant break from—from whatever your normal work happens to be.'

'Very pleasant,' Janie assured her. She had no wish to go into the details of her normal work.

'Unfortunately, this place holds very little to interest a girl of your age. In fact, there's nothing at all.' Penelope's eyes became hard as they flashed an unspoken warning towards Janie.

There was silence in the room until Janie laughed. 'Nothing of interest? What on earth can you mean?'

Penelope shrugged. 'Well, I ask you—what is there?' The dark eyes sent a brief flash towards Lance, then widened as they glared at Janie, almost daring her to admit her interests lay in his direction.

Janie continued to smile. 'From now on there'll be plenty to interest me.' Her gaze went through the window towards the green hills and to where the horses still grazed near the stable yards.

Penelope turned to Lance. 'I'm afraid I don't understand. Didn't you say you intend taking her home on Friday?'

'Only to get extra clothes. Janie is going on the payroll,' he informed her briefly.

'*Payroll!*' Penelope's jaw sagged a fraction. 'I'm afraid I still don't understand——'

'It's the polo ponies,' Janie explained. 'Surely you know about Peter Bryant's accident? He won't be riding for ages and the ponies must be exercised each day so that they'll be fit and ready for play when the season opens in December——'

'Don't you think I know all that?' Penelope cut in angrily, then her tone altered as she turned to Lance. 'Didn't you realise that I could have exercised them for you?'

He returned her look steadily. 'No, I'm not aware that you could have done the job.'

Her voice rose as she tried to control her temper. 'That's quite ridiculous! You know perfectly well that I can ride.'

He regarded her grimly. 'I've watched you on horseback, Penelope. I've seen you wrenching at the horse's mouth. In my opinion, you're far too heavy-handed. I also recall pointing out these things to you, but you've taken little or no notice.'

She glared at him, indignation causing her to open her mouth and then shut it again.

Lance went on relentlessly. 'This job calls for an expert like Janie who has handled polo ponies for years. She's got *hands*.'

Nell, who had been silent for some time now spoke with quiet satisfaction. 'I found Janie for Lance.' She went on to tell Penelope about the days when she had sat with Laura Meredith, while their men had raced up and down the field, swinging mallets in an effort to shoot goals. 'Janie was always in charge of her father's ponies,' she added.

Penelope's lips curled as she stood up abruptly. 'How very nice for her. Well, I'm afraid I must leave. Sam will be coming home from school and I *always* like to be there when he arrives.'

'Except when you're away in Auckland or elsewhere,' Maud put in slyly.

'At least his grandmother is there during those times,' Penelope told Maud coolly. She said goodbye to Nell, but ignored Maud and Janie in her farewell, and then she turned to Lance with a cryptic remark. 'I may not be a good *rider*—but at least I'm a good *mother*. You don't always find *both* virtues wrapped up in one body, so you have to decide which is the more important.'

'I'll see you to your car,' Lance said gruffly.

Their departure left a silence in the room, until Janie was unable to suppress a sigh as she said, 'I've a strong feeling that Penelope dislikes me.'

Maud gave a short laugh. 'So that makes two of us.' She began to carry the afternoon teacups and saucers towards the dishwasher.

Nell drew her spinning-wheel from its corner. 'This is what I need—it's so soothing,' she told them.

Janie glanced from one to the other. 'Isn't there anything I can do for either of you? I'm free until the ponies have to be fed.' Privately, she wondered when Lance would return to the room.

The wheel turned as Nell treadled rhythmically. She smiled at Janie and said, 'Yes, there is one small task you could do for us both. There are some skeins of wool that have been washed and are now waiting to be rolled into balls. I'm sure you know how to cope with that particular chore.'

'Only too well. Where are they?'

'Hanging on a line in the laundry,' Nell said. 'The cream ones are mine and the grey ones are Maud's.'

'I'll find them,' Janie promised. She made her way to the laundry, which was equipped with an automatic-machine, a clothes dryer and two stainless-steel tubs. The skeins of homespun wool hung from a line stretching across the room near the window, and, glancing through it, the sight of the yellow car still in the yard made her pause.

Penelope was behind the wheel, while Lance sat beside her in the passenger seat. He appeared to be speaking earnestly, as though explaining something of a serious nature and, watching them, Janie was assailed by the suspicion that it concerned herself. Was it necessary, she wondered, for Lance to give further explanation for her own presence in the house? What subject other than that of another woman could place such a sulky expression on Penelope's face? Also, was the situation between them deeper than either Nell or Maud suspected?

A sudden fear that she could be observed watching them,

made her snatch the skeins from the line, and moments later she was back in the living-room, where she found that Maud had placed a wool-winding device on the table. Its revolving, outstretched arms waited for a skein to be placed over them, and as Janie rolled the first one into a ball her thoughts were still with the couple in the car.

A short time later, Nell complained plaintively, 'I must be going deaf. I haven't heard Penelope's car leave, and I always hear her revving the motor.'

'Nonsense, dear, you're not deaf,' Maud assured her. 'It's just that she hasn't left yet.'

Janie was well aware of this fact, but she said nothing as she made determined efforts to keep her eyes from straying towards the door, while hoping and waiting for Lance to return to the room. However, it was at least ten minutes before the yellow car swept along the drive, and although the sound of it lifted her spirits, Lance did not make an appearance. Nor could she understand why such a small detail should cause her to feel so very disappointed.

She did not see him until she went out to feed the horses, and she then noticed he had little to say. He seemed remote and deep in thought, and she felt sure it had something to do with the conversation that had taken place in Penelope's car.

As soon as the horses had been rugged and turned out for the night, she ran back to the house, then went upstairs, where she showered and changed into her jade check dress with the buttoned cuffs and cravat-style neck. She took special care with her make-up, and when she returned to the living-room Maud looked at her approvingly.

'Now that's what I call a most attractive dress—and much more feminine than closely fitting riding pants,' the older woman whispered in her ear.

But if Lance noticed the change in her apearance he gave no sign. He poured the pre-dinner sherries, and as he handed a crystal glass to Janie she imagined his eyes held a question.

Nor did he have much to say during the meal, although Janie tried to break some of his long silences by talking about the polo ponies. 'Tomorrow I shall take photographs of them,' she said.

He looked at her thoughtfully. 'Do you always carry a camera?'

'Of course. Father gave it to me soon after he'd given me my portable typewriter——' She stopped, fearful that the subject could lead her on to dangerous ground.

'I didn't think short stories warranted photography,' Lance said, his eyes penetrating. 'They're only fiction, aren't they?'

'Half the world carries a camera,' Nell reminded him. 'You must show Janie the photos you brought home from overseas.'

'Yes, well—we'll have to think about that.' He sent a hard stare across the table towards Janie. 'You'd be interested in some of my overseas polo photos?'

Instinct warned her to be wary. 'Only if you feel inclined to show them to me,' she responded with casual indifference. 'Otherwise—it doesn't matter.'

'Hmm. Well, as I said—we'll have to think about it.'

Nell leaned forward. 'What is there to think about? Why don't you show them to Janie this evening?' she suggested brightly.

'Why?' His mouth tightened as he looked from one to the other. 'Because I'm going out.'

He made no explanation as to where he'd be going, nor did anyone voice a question. However, it was easy to guess he'd be going to see Penelope.

Janie's eyes held undisguised curiosity as they rested upon him. Was this the man who had kissed her this morning? Was he the same person who had held her against him while the rain had pattered on the haybarn roof? For some strange reason, his attitude towards herself appeared to have taken on a subtle change. Thinking about it, she became obsessed with the feeling that the cause had something to do with Penelope's visit.

Pride came to her rescue when she was forced to suppress a yawn which enabled her to say with all sincerity, 'I'm afraid I wouldn't be very interested in looking at photos this evening. It's ages since I've done so much riding and I'm rather tired, so—if you'll excuse me—I'll go to bed early.'

Later she heard Lance's car leave the garage and, after a short period of watching television, she climbed the stairs to her bedroom. Lying in the darkness, she wondered about his unexpected coolness where she herself was concerned, but her ponderings did not last long, because within a short time she was asleep.

The next morning she was out at the stable by eight o'clock, and again Lance was there before her. He greeted her cheerfully, appearing to have shaken off whatever irritating thoughts had plagued him the previous evening. Nevertheless, she kept her distance from him, and when he drew near to her in the stable she skipped out of reach. There would be no repetition of yesterday's embraces, she told herself firmly.

As they prepared to leave the stable yard, Lance said, 'We'll take a different route from yesterday. I want to examine the boundary fence, to make sure it's in order.'

'"Good boundary fences keep good relations between neighbours,"' Janie smiled, quoting a phrase often uttered by her father.

'It'll be a hilly ride,' he warned.

Was he avoiding the haybarn? she wondered, her eyes taking in the virility of his form as he mounted grey Dandy and prepared to lead Major. She herself rode Joy and led Gay, and as they left the yard she scanned the sky for a hint of rain. White clouds scudded across the blue, but none appeared to be in danger of dropping a deluge.

The route took them round the outskirts of the property and, as Lance led the way along the most suitable tracks for the horses, she had no option but to follow Major. It meant there was little opportunity for conversation as they rode but, after all, she reminded herself, they were there to exercise the horses rather than to fill the air with chatter.

Some of the inland hills rose steeply before dropping to flat areas where red Hereford cattle grazed in lush grass, but eventually the route led them towards the coastal boundaries of the property. And although the land now fell towards the sea there were still areas where cliffs rose above the rocky shore.

Here they were able to ride abreast and, turning to look at her critically, Lance said, 'Your cheeks are glowing. Could it be that you are enjoying yourself?'

'It's really the sea breeze, although I'll admit I'm loving every moment of riding on these hills.' She looked away from him as she thought, Not to mention riding with you. Then, almost betraying this fact, she added, 'I can't expect you to be riding with me every day.'

'No, but I shall do so until you've learnt the geography of the property. Then it'll be necessary for you to take the ponies a pair at a time. Are you sure it won't be too boring?'

'Of course not, but I'll miss your company.' The words slipped out before she could stop them.

But apparently he attached no importance to the admission, his deep chuckle almost brushing it away. 'I doubt it. I'm sure you'll spend your time thinking up plots for short stories.'

'It's possible,' she said, knowing that some form of mental control would be necessary to keep her thoughts from constantly dwelling upon him. And then a figure in the distance caught her attention and, pointing to it, she was glad to be able to change the subject. 'Is that somebody working away over there?'

He followed the direction of her gaze. 'Yes—it's Don Watson. You met him at the haybarn—remember?'

She was unable to look at him. 'Yes, I remember.' But it seemed the haybarn had no significant memory for him, because he said lightly, 'Don is moving part of the fence back from where the land near it is beginning to fall away.'

'Oh.' She peeped to find him staring straight ahead. So their kisses and the closeness of their bodies when in the haybarn had been merely an incident to be forgotten. Then, taking a deep breath, she controlled her disappointment by asking, 'Where does Don live?'

'With Sid Brown and his wife. He has a flat attached to their house, and he can either have meals with them or fend for himself. Normally, Peter Bryant shares it with him.'

They found Don busily digging a posthole, his motorcycle propped on its support a short distance away, while nearby lay battens, a box of staples and a roll of fencing wire. He straightened his back as they approached, grinned broadly with his eyes on Janie and said, 'Hi, boss—good day, Miss Meredith.'

Janie dismounted while the work was being discussed. She tethered Gay and Joy to the fence, where the cliff edge was a safe distance away, then walked to where she could gaze down upon the sea breaking over the rocks. But the white foam dashing across the dark masses had a frightening effect, causing her to draw back, and bringing to mind the fact that her mother had said Lance's father had met his death in some such place.

She shuddered as she returned to the horses, but as she rejoined Lance and Don her mind became alert as she caught the trend of their conversation. Apparently, it concerned Penelope's son, Sam.

Don was saying, 'I didn't want to tell tales on the boy, but

I thought you ought to know, and I felt that Sid was the one to tell you. After all, he's the manager here, and that's why he phoned and said he wanted to have a chat.'

Lance nodded. 'I understand. You were quite right.'

'It seems to me the lad has the run of the place—almost as if he lives here. And boys will be boys—one can't let them get away with too much.' Don's suntanned face showed concern.

Lance frowned. 'I suppose it's my fault. No doubt I've been too lenient with him.'

'Well, it's probably difficult to be tough with him— especially when you're so matey with his mother——'

Lance glared at him coldly, a steely glint creeping into his eyes.

Don put his foot in even further. 'Well, I mean you've known her for years—childhood sweethearts and all that sort of thing—and now they say there's talk of you and her getting together——' He faltered and fell silent.

'*They?* Who are *they?*' Lance snapped.

'I think it's mainly the fellows working on her father's place——'

Janie came to Don's rescue. 'Is young Sam in trouble?' she asked, amused by the flush that had risen to his face.

Don snatched at the opportunity to talk to her. 'I'll say he is! I caught the little devil up in the hayloft above the stable. He had a box of matches and a candle, if you please. The whole place could have gone up in smoke.'

Janie was shocked. 'Surely he's too young to be playing with such dangerous things as *matches?*'

'He's got what he calls a fort up there,' Don explained. 'It's built out of the remaining bales of hay that he's been able to push and shove into position. But the light is dim because the front top door is locked and the skylight is covered with cobwebs. So what does he do? He finds a candle and grabs a box of matches, and up he goes to sit in his fort with a book. Quiet as a mouse, he was—reading by candlelight.'

'How did you find him?' Janie asked. The thought of Sam in the hayloft with matches and candle gave her the horrors.

'I happened to go into the stable and I heard coughing. Some of the dust must have got down his throat. Anyhow, Sid and Mr Winter had a good long chat about it last night——'

Janie shot a quick glance towards Lance, but made no comment. The realisation that he had not visited Penelope last evening leapt into her mind, and suddenly the day seemed to be brighter. At the same time, she paused to ask herself why this should be. Surely she wasn't allowing the magnetism of this man to wrap itself around her?

They continued the ride, which was now homeward, and when they came to the haybarn he drew rein while turning to look at her. The action caused an inner fluttering somewhere near her heart, and she wondered if he intended to refer to yesterday's episode. Her cheeks felt hot as she waited for him to speak, but his words came as an anticlimax.

'Do you think you could do the poles alone this afternoon?'

'Yes, of course.' She was conscious of disappointment, but she kept her tone light as she added, 'I'll take them one by one from the stable yard.'

He nodded approval. 'I've decided to go in search of the shearers. I'd like to know how far they've got with the flocks on their list.'

'Do you know where to find them?'

'A few phone calls will tell me whose flock they're working on at present, and how long it will be before they come to us—weather permitting, of course.'

'Shearing is so dependent upon the weather,' she sighed,

wishing he would ask her to go with him. Although she waited hopefully, the invitation did not come.

But, after all, why should she expect it? She was there to exercise the polo ponies, wasn't she? And, apart from her ability to do that, he'd shown little real interest in her company, or in herself for that matter. Oh, yes, he had kissed her, but what did that mean? Obviously nothing at all, because he was no doubt in the habit of kissing Penelope as well.

And then light dawned. *Of course*—he'd be taking Penelope with him. How could she have been foolish enough to have imagined otherwise? Take a grip on your common sense, stupid, she told herself. Snap out of this obsession of wanting to be with him.

And suddenly her eyes widened from shock, as the truth dawned clearly. Therein lay her whole trouble. Despite the short time she had known him—*she wanted to be with him.*

CHAPTER FIVE

THE disturbing knowledge was hammered home even more firmly during the afternoon when Janie rode alone. Although the task of riding each horse along the farm road, and then zigzagging for a period between the poles, required her concentration to a certain degree, there was one small part of her mind that kept searching for Lance.

She knew it was ridiculous to keep listening for his voice, and quite insane to scan the countryside in the hope of seeing him come riding over the hills. It all added up to a bad bout of wishful thinking, and to the fact that she was missing him abominably. To make matters worse, she knew she'd have to become used to it.

Matters didn't improve when she rode Major. Head-shaking tactics from the bay gelding told her he knew somebody different held the reins, but he settled down when he recognised an experienced rider on his back. 'I know how you feel,' she consoled, patting his neck. 'We both miss him—and that's a fact.'

She worked with the horses until late in the afternoon, Dandy being the last to be put through his paces at the poles, and by that time she was weary and in need of a cup of good hot tea. She turned him loose into the paddock, and as she carried the saddle towards the stable doors her attention was caught by the sound of a soft whinny.

She paused to look about her, then realised it had not come from Dandy, nor had it come from the other horses now grazing in the paddock. Had it come from behind the stable? She placed the saddle on the ground while she walked to the rear of the building, and there, tethered to a rail, stood Tinker, the Shetland pony.

It could only mean that Sam was in the vicinity—perhaps up in the hayloft. She returned to the front entrance, put the saddle on its rack, then made her way quietly up the stairs. At the top, she was greeted by a faint glow of candlelight coming from an alcove of hay bales, and within the circle of illumination sat Sam, his head bent over a book.

The sight brought a sharp exclamation of fear from her. 'Sam! You've no right to be up here with a candle—it's *dangerous*!'

He looked up and stared at her, wisps of dark hair falling across his eye. 'It's not dangerous, because I'm careful.'

'You could have an accident—you could knock the candle over——'

'Of course I wouldn't do anything like that!' His voice was scathing. 'I'm eight now, and that's dumb baby stuff.'

'Anyone can have an accident,' she pointed out.

'Not me,' he declared stubbornly.

Janie looked at him thoughtfully, wondering if she could reason with him in a friendly manner. 'Don found you up here,' she reminded him. 'Didn't he say you were not to do this?'

'*Don!* I don't take notice of *him*. Mum says he's only *staff*. He can't tell me what to do. I only take notice of Uncle Lance.'

'Uncle Lance would be furious if he could see you up here with a lighted candle.'

'I bet he wouldn't. Uncle Lance knows I'm careful. He lets me go anywhere I want to. When I live here, I bet he lets me sleep up in this loft—right here in my fort.'

Janie was interested. 'Oh? Are you coming to live here?'

'Yeah.'

'When will that be?' she asked, almost fearing the answer.

'When Mum and Uncle Lance get married, of course.'

Janie's heart almost stood still. 'But—when will that be?'

Sam shook his head. 'I dunno—but Grandma says it's *high time*.

'Grandma wants them to get married?' Janie asked in a low voice.

'Yeah. She says the sooner the better. When I grow up, I'll work on this place. I'll be the boss.'

'Oh? What about Uncle Lance? Won't he be here?'

'He'll be too old,' Sam said decisively. 'I bet he'll be forty. He'll just sit in the sun like Grandpa.'

Janie began to giggle at the thought of Lance just sitting in the sun. 'You're saying he'll be pensioned off?'

'I dunno. What's "pensioned off" mean?'

'You'll understand some day, Sam—but in the mean time you're coming down out of this loft and you'll bring your candle and matches with you.'

'You can't boss me,' he declared loudly.

'No? Then I'll have to go and find Uncle Lance, and if he doesn't put a flea in your ear I'll be most surprised.'

'You're a big Tell-Tale-Tit!' Sam shouted at her. 'Tell-Tale-Tit, your tongue shall be slit, and all the dogs in the town shall have a little bit!' His face had become red with fury.

Janie became exasperated. 'Listen to me, Sam. Uncle Lance already knows about your antics up here and he's very annoyed about it.'

'I bet Don told him.' The boy's eyes glittered angrily.

'Don told Mr Brown—and he was quite right to do so. They probably think you should be banned from the property. Do you know what banned means?' she added as an afterthought.

'I'm not sure. You tell me.'

'It means that Uncle Lance might give orders for you not to come to Golden Hills at all.'

'Huh! He wouldn't do that, because he's gonna marry Mum.' Sam was full of confidence.

'He might change his mind about that, too,' Janie warned quietly.

Sam's eyes became round as he digested this remark in silence.

Janie sensed she'd played a trump card. 'He won't want to become saddled with a boy who's disobedient and troublesome,' she added, pressing home the advantage. 'Somebody likely to burn down the stable.'

Sam blew out the candle, then scrambled to his feet. 'I better be going home,' he mumbled.

'A good idea,' Janie agreed. 'Don't forget your book—and the matches,' she added as an afterthought, as she followed him down the stairs and to the back of the stable. Moments later, she watched him canter away on Tinker.

When she returned to the front of the building, she realised the horses were grouped at the gate and waiting to enter the yard for their evening feed. She let them in, gave each one its ration of oats and chaff, then put on the night rugs.

Lance arrived as she was fastening Major's last buckle. 'How did you manage at the poles?' he asked, running critical eyes over the horses.

'No trouble at all. Everything went well,' she assured him. 'Did you find the shearers?'

'Oh, yes—quite easily. They hope to be here next week.'

'I suppose Penelope knew where to find them. I presume she was with you?' Shut up, you fool, she hissed at herself.

Ignoring the question, he moved towards the stable. 'Speaking of Penelope reminds me of young Sam. Was he in residence today? I thought I'd take a look at his fort.'

'Yes, he was up there this afternoon,' she admitted reluctantly, deciding it would be unwise to shield the boy's activities from Lance.

She followed him up the stairs, then watched as he found a broom and swept the two skylights free of cobwebs. Their removal enabled more light to filter into the loft and, when he opend the door to the narrow outside platform, rays from the setting sun shot golden shafts through the disturbed dust.

Outside the door and jutting from beneath the gable above, was a strong bracket with rope and hook attached, its purpose being to draw bales of hay up into the loft. And as she gazed at it Janie was reminded of childhood days, when she had watched men loading the loft above the stable at home. A wave of nostalgia shook her, causing her to blink rapidly, until Lance's voice spoke sharply.

'Come away from that door. I hate to see people standing near the edge of a drop.' His hand on her arm drew her away from the opening, but instead of releasing it he drew her closer to him.

She leaned against him without resistance, then said shakily, 'Did you think I was about to leap out?'

'I didn't like the expression on your face. It held a depth of unhappiness.'

'I—I was remembering some of my younger days. It was the sight of that bracket and hook. It made me see bales of hay being lifted up—and I could see my father standing at the door above——'

His hand stroked her head as it rested against his shoulder. 'At least you never saw him lying dead on rocks at the foot of a cliff.'

She was shocked. 'Is that how you remember your father?'

'Yes, unfortunately—although we were lucky to find him before the tide came in.'

She looked up at him, her eyes filled with distress. 'What happened? Can you bear to talk about it?'

'It was years ago—and now it's no more than a ghastly

nightmare that flashes back into my memory at odd times.
We really don't know what happened. We could only
presume he'd gone to the edge of the cliff to rescue a sheep,
because there was a dead ewe lying near him. Sometimes
they push through the fence and then find their way down
to a ledge from which they're unable to get back.'

'The grass on the other side is always greener.'

'Exactly.' He was silent for several moments before going
on bitterly, 'To add to our trauma, we discovered there
were those who suggested he'd commited suicide because it
was well known he'd never really got over my mother's
death.'

She gave a deep sigh. 'You've had your share of sadness.'
Her voice was full of understanding as, still leaning against
him, her arms went round his waist. It was really a gesture
of sympathy, but it had a reaction as his head bent and his
lips found her own.

Time seemed to stand still for Janie, as she gave herself
up to the bliss of Lance's kiss. She felt his fingers threading
through the thickness of her golden hair, gently twisting
the ends into curls. They moved to fondle an ear, feather-
light on the lobe, before tracing their way to a vulnerable
nerve near her throat.

Her pulses began to throb, causing her lips to part as his
kiss deepened to betray the fervour of his rising emotion.
She became aware of vibrations quivering through her
body—sensations to which she was unaccustomed, and she
knew a wild joy that caused her to cling to him in a manner
that was completely abandoned. She didn't have the power
to protest when he swept her up into his arms and carried
her towards a pile of hay that had been pushed together
from several broken bales.

Lowering her gently into its softness, he stretched his
length beside her, then leaned on one elbow to gaze down
into her face. His eyes lit by an inner fire, he murmured

huskily, 'Blue-eyes, you're so very beautiful. Do you have to be told that I want you—that I need you?'

Janie could only stare at him wordlessly.

He continued to gaze into her eyes, almost as if probing beyond them and into her mind. His voice still husky, he said, 'If you're honest, you'll admit you want us to make love——'

Her heart leapt, but still she said nothing.

'Your body is screaming for us to be together,' he pursued relentlessly, his lips against her throat. Then, raising his head to look at her, he murmured, 'Go on—tell me the truth.'

But she was unable to meet his eyes and, turning away, she whispered, 'I didn't say so——'

'You, don't have to. I can feel you calling to me loud and clear.'

A denial rose to her lips, but before it could be uttered his mouth possessed hers again. His arms moved to crush her against the hardness of his body, nor were words needed to tell her of the raging desire that flamed through his entire being.

Responding, her arms wound about his neck, and as her own mounting desire rose to meet his an assortment of strange thoughts snaked through her mind. Bells seemed to ring in her head, causing her to wonder if she could really hear them, or were they a figment of her imagination?

Bells. You give yourself to a man only when you hear bells, someone had once told her. But were these warning bells, or wedding bells, that rang in her fancy? Then, as if in answer, Sam's words echoed in her mind, tolling the end to any hopes that might have begun to simmer in her mind. *When Mum and Uncle Lance get married*, he had said.

The memory had the effect of a cold shower. She almost felt the blood drain from her face, and a sudden shudder passed through her.

Lance was quick to sense her changed attitude. 'What's the matter?' he demanded.

She shook her head as she removed her arms from about his neck. 'I—I think it's time we cooled off——'

His eyes glinted from between narrowed lids. 'What's brought about this abrupt decision?'

'It's—it's just something I remembered.' Her hands pushed against his chest.

'Remembered? Such as what?' he rasped.

She realised she'd better be more definite, therefore she sat up to brush straw from her hair and clothes. 'If you must know, it was something Sam said.'

'Sam? Hell's teeth! What the devil could Sam say that would force you to wriggle out of my arms?'

She turned to stare at him, her eyes wide with accusation. 'Sam is looking forward to the time when you and his mother are married,' she told him quietly. 'He's only a little boy, but obviously he's old enough to know there's an understanding between you and Penelope.'

He stood up and brushed himself clean of loose hay. 'I can hardly believe what I'm hearing! You're insinuating that I'm to marry Penelope—and that in the mean time I'm hankering after a roll in the hay with you?'

'Are you engaged to Penelope?' she demanded bluntly.

'No, I am not engaged to Penelope.' The words were clipped.

'But—you have an understanding of some sort?' she persisted.

'Apparently there are people who imagine this to be the case.'

She waited for him to make further denial of an agreement between them, but it did not come. Instead, he went to the open doors at the end of the loft, pulled them shut with a bang and dropped the bar that held them in place.

Watching him, she said, 'The ponies will have finished their oats and chaff. I'll let them out of the yard.'

'What's the hurry?'

But she felt unable to trust herself alone in the semi-gloom with him, therefore she hurried towards the stairs and almost ran down them to the yard.

The horses were out in the paddock before Lance came down from the loft, and she could only presume he'd taken time to examine Sam's arrangement of bales for his fort. Or was he just standing up there, brooding over her own rejection of him? Perhaps this was his way of telling her he was annoyed.

I'm sorry, Mr Winter—I've no intention of becoming your temporary plaything, she told him mentally. Then, without waiting for him to appear, she ran back to the house ahead of him.

Nell and Maud were in the kitchen when she slipped in and made her way upstairs to her bedroom. She showered and changed into a pale green dress of fine-knitted rib, and as she buckled its wide gold belt she paused to stare at her face in the mirror. Her cheeks still held a slight flush and her eyes sparkled as though suppressed excitement lurked within her.

'You're still up in the loft with him,' she whispered to her reflection accusingly. 'You're still in his arms. It's written all over your face. You'd better simmer down before he sets eyes on you, or he'll guess the truth. He'll *know* you're longing to be held closely again.'

But despite Janie's efforts to remain calm her inner glow did not escape Maud's sharp eyes. 'You're looking very bright this evening,' the older woman remarked as she served vegetables at the dinner table. 'You must have had a special day.'

'Or has something really amused you?' Lance cut in softly, his dark hazel eyes holding a strangely bleak expression as they surveyed Janie.

The flush in her cheeks deepened. She found herself unable to look at him, but knowing a reply was expected she ignored his question as she turned to Maud. 'It was exhilarating. The ponies seemed to enjoy the poles, and Major didn't want to stop. He could have gone on and on— in and out from left to right——'

'You must have had him hypnotised,' Lance remarked drily, still watching her closely.

Nell sent Janie a satisfied smile. 'I'm glad you can manage Major. He's Lance's favourite, although he can be very stroppy at times.' She turned to her nephew. 'What's on television tonight? Have you looked at the paper?'

He shook his head. 'No, I shan't be watching TV this evening. I'm going out.'

'Oh.' Nell looked disappointed. 'You were out last night,' she reminded him.

He sent her a smile that did not quite reach his eyes. 'If you must know my movements, Nell—I'm going to visit Penelope.'

Nell and Maud stared at him with eyes that were full of reproach. Neither of them spoke and the silence became tense, until Janie forced herself to smile at him. 'Of course you must go and see her—even if she did go driving with you this afternoon——' She stopped abruptly, suddenly afraid of the words that were ready to come tumbling forth. Jealousy raged within her, but she hadn't realised it had reached the stage of causing her to lose control of her tongue.

Lance glared at her. 'If you *must* know, Penelope was *not* with me this afternoon. However, there are matters to be discussed.'

'Oh, yes, I suppose so.' Her earlier exhilaration had vanished with surprising speed, and her eyes held questions as she looked at him. He was not engaged to Penelope, he'd said—but was it closer than he had admitted? The thought of it gave her pain, and this in itself was also something for her to think about. Was it any concern of hers if Lance decided to marry Penelope? No, of course it wasn't. Nor had she the right to be consumed by this dreadful jealousy that positively gnawed at her.

His next words caught her attention. 'Actually, I have a matter to discuss with young Sam,' he informed Nell and Maud. 'He appears to have taken up residence in the stable loft.'

'Has he permission to go there?' Maud asked.

Lance shrugged. 'Not really—but boys will be boys. Some build huts up in tress, others have dug-outs in the side of a cliff or hill. Sam prefers to read in the warmth and comfort of hay.'

Maud frowned. 'If you want my personal opinion, I consider you're too soft with him. He does just as he likes round this place. I've even caught him helping himself from the cake tins——'

Nell smiled understandingly. 'He certainly loves your chocolate cake, Maud. Oh, well, I don't suppose he can do any harm up in the stable loft——'

'Not unless he accidentally knocks over the candle,' Janie was unable to resist adding to Nell's remark. Her words were really meant to remind Lance of the danger, and while she knew he was not entirely stupid, she could also see that he was far too tolerant towards the boy. But no doubt this stemmed from his feelings for Penelope.

The statement brought forth cries of horror. *'Candles! Matches!'* came from Maud.

'Oh, Lance! He's only eight. You can't allow him to take such dangerous things up into the loft!' Nell exclaimed.

'OK—OK——' he soothed. 'The subject will be discussed, not only with the mother, but with the young man himself.'

Janie looked down at her plate. She could imagine Lance reprimanding the boy—and then settling down to a long, cosy chat with his mother. The thought sent a chill through her body, and as soon as dinner was over she went upstairs to find something warm to wrap round her shoulders.

The cream woollen batwing cardigan she put on had been spun and knitted by her mother, and as she fastened the front buttons she wandered out on to the balcony. Shafts of light shining through the doors of Lance's room told her he was getting ready to go out, and she was about to return through her own door when his voice caused her to pause.

'Janine, just a moment—you didn't answer my question.' He strode along the balcony to face her.

Janine, she noticed, looking at him blankly, then asked, 'What question are you talking about?'

'The one I put to you at the dinner table, and which you so deftly pushed aside. I asked if something had really amused you. Please don't try to tell me you can't remember.'

'I—I'm afraid I don't understand,' she hedged.

'Oh yes, you do.' He glared at her coldly. 'Wasn't it our little episode up in the loft that gave you so much amusement? You allowed me to think you were responding—that you felt as I did—but in actual fact you were merely giving yourself a good laugh. And when you came downstairs for dinner you were still giggling inside.'

She was appalled by his words. 'No, you're quite wrong!' she gasped, longing to throw herself into his arms and to assure him that such was not the case.

'That's the way I read the situation,' he gritted.

'Then it's time you learnt to read more clearly,' she snapped as, frustrated, she glanced at her wristwatch and added, 'Won't you be late? Penelope will be wondering where you are. She'll be waiting for you.'

His face became a cold mask as he stared at her for

several long moments before he turned swiftly and strode back into his room.

Tears welled into her eyes as the slam of his door echoed in her ears. How could he possibly think she'd been *laughing* at him? Couldn't he understand that her exuberance had been born of an inner joy—and from the sheer happiness of having been held in his arms? But those moments were delicious memories she'd be wiser to wipe from her mind because, obviously, his thoughts were with Penelope.

In fact, her wisest plan would be to leave this place before she found herself hopelessly in love with this devastating man who had the power to make her pulses thump and who seemed to be creeping slowly and surely into her system. *Slowly?* Good grief, she had known him for little more than a couple of days!

Impulse made her drag her suitcase from the back of the wardrobe, but even as she began to throw clothes into it a vision of the four polo ponies rose before her eyes. She enjoyed handling the fillies, Gay and Joy, and, while Major and Dandy had characteristics of their own, they were friendly towards her. They responded towards her in a way that made her recall her father's words.

Horses *know* people, he'd always declared. They know if a person is nervous of them—and they know if a person can master them. And, even as she thought of the ponies responding to her, she found herself responding to life at Golden Hills.

The knowledge made her pause in the act of folding a dress and, leaving it on the bed, she went out to the balcony to breathe in the tangy sea air. Moonlight glowed on this stretch of the South Pacific Ocean, while the hill country lay silhouetted against the stars.

'You can't leave this place just yet,' she whispered to herself. 'Besides, how would you explain your departure to Nell? As for Maud, she would guess at once. She'd know you've become emotionally affected by Lance.' The thoughts were enough to make her replace her dress in the wardrobe and empty the suitcase.

When she went down to the living-room, the two older women were busy with their spinning-wheels. The television offered distraction, but did not stop their work, because both were sufficiently expert to throw glances at the screen while the spun wool found its way on to the bobbin.

Nell's wheel became still as Janie entered the room and sat on a chair between them. Her grey eyes were a little troubled as she said, 'I'm so sorry Lance has seen fit to go out *again*, dear. He was out *last* evening.'

Janie's brows rose as she feigned surprise. 'Oh? Did you want him to stay at home for some special reason?'

Nell avoided her eyes as she reached into a basket of wool. The handful she picked up had been carded into a soft fluffy mass, and as she drew fine strands from it she admitted, 'Yes, well—I hoped you could have spent a pleasant evening together. I'd like you to really *know* each other.'

A shaky laugh escaped Janie. 'He's probably had enough of my company for one day. We spent hours together this morning. Besides——' She fell silent as she thought of the time they'd spent in the loft, her eyes clouding as she wondered if Lance would hold Penelope as closely as he'd held herself.

Maud was watching her. 'Yes? Besides what?' she probed, leaving her chair to turn down the volume of the television.

Janie thought quickly. 'Besides—he must talk to Penelope about Sam's activities in the loft,' she reminded them. 'I feel sure that's the real reason for his visit to her this evening.' Although that's a clear bout of wishful thinking on my part, she added silently to herself.

Maud looked at her anxiously. 'You don't think there's anything more to it?'

'I don't know.' Janie thought for a moment before she added, 'Perhaps I should warn you that Sam expects to live here when his mum and Uncle Lance get married.' She told them of her conversation with the boy in the loft.

Nell and Maud listened with visible signs of dismay. 'That means there's *talk* of it, at least,' the former quavered in a plaintive voice. 'Maud, dear, what shall we do?'

'You will begin by not upsetting yourself,' Maud declared in a firm voice. 'Janie was quite right to warn us, but it's possible nothing will ever come of it. Of course Lance has to talk to Penelope about the boy striking matches in the loft.'

'It's easy to see her mother's point of view,' Nell persisted with agitation. 'Naturally, she's pushing for it. It would ensure that her daughter would be nicely close at hand if Penelope married Lance.'

'For heaven's sake—stop worrying about it,' Maud said sharply.

But the situation continued to nag at Nell's mind until, almost desperately, she turned to Janie with a wild plea. 'My dear—oh, my dear—if only you'd grab Lance by the scruff of the neck and drag him off to the altar——'

Janie gaped at her speechlessly until she said, 'You're joking, of course.'

'No, indeed I am not,' Nell declared vehemently. 'I mean every word of it.'

'Nell, dear, you're being unwise,' Maud warned. 'You're rushing matters. Give Janie a chance. She's known Lance for less than a week. You wouldn't want to see her marry in haste and repent at Golden Hills.'

Nell looked at Maud in a dazed way, then appeared to come to her senses. 'No, of course not, although I can't see how anyone could repent through marrying Lance. He's—

he's such a—a *wonderful* person——'

Janie eased the situation with a light laugh. 'He must have faults tucked away somewhere,' she suggested.

'What man hasn't?' Maud queried briskly, then she smiled. 'Nell, dear—we *know* how you feel about Lance. For years you've been his aunt, mother, grandmother—the lot, rolled into one. Even if you could *see* his faults you'd *never* admit to them.'

Nell was startled by the accusation. 'Surely I'm not quite so daft?' She turned to Janie. 'Do you think I'm obsessed to that extent? Now, tell me honestly.'

Janie grinned at her. 'There are millions of mothers who consider there isn't a girl good enough for their precious son.'

'And you think I'm one of them?' Nell's voice was querulous.

'It's possible you could stand in line with them. It's enough to make any girl hesitate before grabbing him by the scruff of the neck and dragging him to the altar,' she added, laughing as she threw Nell's words back at her.

But Nell was not amused. 'In all seriousness, Janie, dear—if you could possibly bring yourself to love Lance sufficiently to marry him—I'd be most grateful.'

Janie's eyes widened. 'Do you realise what you're saying? Do you really mean those words?'

Nell straightened her back as she stared at Janie. 'Of course I mean them. Why do you think I invited you to come here? You're a sweet, beautiful girl—born of good parents. You're most suitable and nothing would make me happier than to see——' She paused to gaze hopefully at Janie.

Maud said, 'Ah, now we *are* coming out into the open. You're a deep one, Nell, but actually I was beginning to guess——'

Nell ignored the comment as she leaned eagerly towards

Janie, 'So, if Lance comes to his senses——'

'Before Penelope's got him roped and hogtied,' Maud cut in drily.

'Please don't refuse him,' Nell finished, appeal written all over her face and ringing in her voice.

Janie looked at her steadily. 'It's gratifying to know that you'd approve of me as a wife for Lance, but there's one point you appear to have forgotten.'

'And that is——' Nell looked at her anxiously.

'It's manners to wait till I'm asked—and I'm afraid that will never happen.'

'*Afraid?* Then you do like him?'

But before Janie could find an answer the faint thud of a lowered garage door came to their ears. It heralded Lance's return, and moments later he walked into the room.

Nell looked at him fondly. 'You're not very late, dear. We didn't expect you to come home for *hours.*'

His dark brows rose. 'Really? Does this mean you've taken to timing my movements?'

'Of course not,' Nell assured him hastily. She paused before asking pleasantly, 'How is Penelope's mother? I hope she's well.'

'I think so—and even more charming than usual.'

'And her father?' Maud asked. 'The last time I spoke to him, I wondered if he has a drinking problem.'

'When would that have been?' Lance turned to regard Maud.

'He came here last Wednesday morning to see if our gardener could give him a few extra days. I could smell drink on him—and in the *morning*, if you please.'

'*Disgusting!*' Nell exclaimed.

'He's asked me to supervise the property for him,' Lance informed them casually.

Maud sent him a swift glance of surprise. 'But he has a manager.'

'Yes, but it's a matter of making sure the manager is taking the right course.'

'What's wrong with his own supervision?' Nell demanded.

Lance shrugged. 'It's possible he's losing confidence in his own judgement. He wants someone to lean on.'

'So, what's your decision?' Maud asked, staring at Lance.

'I said I'd think about it,' he told her coolly.

She continued to stare at him. 'Of course, you know what it will *mean*, and no doubt it's what *they* have in mind.'

'Mean? You tell me. What will it mean, Maud?' His voice was tinged with amusement.

'Well, naturally, it'll mean you'll have to spend a great deal of time there,' she pointed out.

Nell raised troubled eyes to his face. 'Maud's right. You'll have to be there much more often than you are now. Haven't you enough to do without all that extra work, Lance?'

He made no reply.

In the silence that followed Nell's words Janie found the opportunity to voice a question that had been filling her mind. 'Did you——' she began, but her query died on her lips as, turning to him, she was surprised to find his eyes resting upon her, a strange expression lurking within their depths. She could only ponder its meaning, wondering if his visit to Penelope had caused another bout of antagonism towards herself. Was it actual antagonism or distrust?

His voice pierced her thoughts. 'Yes? You were about to say something?' His mouth had hardened as he looked at her.

'I wondered if you'd got the message to Sam.'

'I did—and quite definitely.'

'Well, I'd like to know the ruling. Is he allowed up in the loft—or do I send him away if I find him there?'

He gave a short laugh. 'Do you imagine he'd take the

slightest notice of you? He's a determined little boy, whose aim is to do just exactly as he wishes.' He paused, frowning. 'I've a strong suspicion that an argument with Sam was the cause of Peter Bryant's fall down the stairs.'

They looked at him in shocked silence until Janie asked, 'What makes you think so?'

'I asked him if he knew how it had happened. He went crimson and hung his head, refusing to speak. I'll talk to Peter about it.'

'I'm still unaware of the situation,' Janie reminded him.

'The situation is that he's banned from the stable entirely.'

'How did he take it?' Nell asked.

'He bellowed like a young bull and rushed off to bed.'

Janie stood up and smiled at Nell and Maud. 'Bed. That's exactly where I'm going right now. Goodnight—everyone.' She left the room without even glancing at Lance.

As she went up the stairs, she told herself she didn't care about the coolness of his attitude towards her—but this, of course, was a lie. She *did* care—*deeply*. And later, as she lay staring wide-eyed into the darkness, the memory of it wrapped her in a dark blanket of depression.

CHAPTER SIX

JANIE woke next morning to find the sky cloudless, and the air crisp and clear. A sound sleep had done much to banish her gloom of the previous evening, and she ran downstairs in a cheerful mood, ate her breakfast quickly, then hurried out to the stable.

But here she was greeted by the sight of three horses instead of four. Major was missing, and it took several moments before she came to the conclusion that Lance had been there earlier than usual and had ridden away on the bay gelding. The disappointment was intense and, although she scanned the hills for the slightest glimpse of horse and rider, she could see no sign of them.

Her depression returned with the force of a chilly wind that swept along the coast. He's avoiding you, it screamed. He's gone without you, because he has no wish for your company. And then a soft whinny from Dandy made her wonder why Lance hadn't taken the grey gelding with him.

'OK, Dandy—I'll ride you,' she told him as she removed his night rug. 'Shall we take Gay or Joy? Perhaps I could manage them both.'

A short time later, she rode Dandy and led the two fillies along the farm road towards the woolshed, where she fully expected to see Major tethered to the rail; but there was no sign of him and the closed doors indicated that the shed was unoccupied while waiting in readiness for the shearers to arrive.

She continued towards the haybarn and as she drew near to it the sound of a *whack* rang on the air. The familiarity of the ringing echo almost made her gasp, and, turning to where the poles stood in line, she saw Lance swinging a mallet. Relief swept her spirits upward, as she realised he'd gone alone to practise hitting the ball rather than to avoid being with her.

He sent her a cheerful wave, then rode towards her. As he drew near he said, 'Good morning. I wondered when you'd arrive. I felt guilty about leaving Dandy, but I'm glad to see you can manage the three of them.'

'The girls are behaving nicely,' she said, turning to observe the two fillies now quietly cropping the grass. Her delight in seeing him was so strong it made her afraid to look at him. Her eyes would surely betray her inner joy, enabling him to guess he was becoming important to her—but just how important even she feared to ask herself.

Still avoiding his eyes, she gazed at the mallet in his hand, then, searching for something to say, she asked, 'May I feel the weight of your stick? It appears to be different from the ones my father used.'

He handed the stick to her. 'That's quite possible. Since plastic balls have taken the place of wooden ones, the polo sticks have become lighter. That one is made from the Malaysian manu cane—the secret of the success of the stick lying in the cane, which comes to New Zealand from Singapore. The head is made of our own native tawa wood which is proving to be most suitable.'

She listened to the depth of timbre in his voice as he explained the details necessary for a good polo mallet; then, as the fillies became restless, she felt compelled to say, 'The girls are giving me a nudge. I'd better keep moving. By the way, is it still convenient to go to Napier tomorrow?'

'Yes. I have an appointment with my accountant at two-thirty in the afternoon. I presume you've phoned your mother?'

She nodded as she urged Dandy towards the long, easy slope which formed part of the exercise area. Perhaps they'd ride together this afternoon, she thought.

In this she was to be disappointed, because she did not see Lance again before the evening meal.

Watching him across the table, she wondered where he'd spent the time, but to ask such a question was impossible. Of course, he could have been attending to farm matters with Sid or Don—but he could also have been with Penelope. Well, at least they would spend time together tomorrow, even if others were present.

It was ten o'clock before they left next morning. Janie was again wearing her yellow and brown tartan skirt, jerkin and white jersey. As she sat beside Maud in the back seat of the Volvo, she was conscious of an inner exhilaration. In searching for its cause, she told herself it was only a nostalgic spin-off from her earlier life, when a day in the city always caused a flutter of excitement. Or perhaps it was because Lance was about to meet her mother.

Thinking about it, she realised an intangible bond was often formed when one's friends met one's parents. It seemed to bring people closer together, and this, she admitted to herself, was something she was hoping for.

Even as the thought formed in her mind, she looked up to meet his dark hazel eyes in the rear-view mirror. Their sombre expression puzzled her until there was a sudden change when he smiled, causing crinkles to appear at the corners, where tiny white lines betrayed his outdoor life.

The smile transformed his face, and Janie's heart lurched as their gaze lurked for several seconds. A flush began to tinge her cheeks, forcing her to drag her eyes away from his and look towards the range of distant blue mountains. *You're a fool*, she told herself fiercely. And then a spasm of apprehension gripped her, as a chance question came from Nell who was sitting beside Lance.

Sending a glance over her shoulder towards Janie, she

asked, 'Your mother understands we'll pick her up at Westshore?'

'Yes, she expects us about midday.' It was then Janie recalled that, while she had made the arrangements, she had not explained to her mother that all plans for an interview with Lance had been scrapped. Nor had it been possible to do so, because Lance had been near the phone.

Would she be able to whisper a word in mother's ear before questions were voiced about the intended interview? It wouldn't be easy, she feared, visualising their arrival. In her mind's eye, she saw her mother hurry out to greet them, leaving no opportunity to hiss the slightest warning. At the same time, Lance would leave his seat to open the car door.

Mother never failed to show interest in her daughter's activities, and Janie could almost hear the anxious queries tumbling forth. 'Has Lance told you everything you wanted to know, dear? Did you remember all the questions you wanted to ask? Have you written the polo article yet? You did take your portable typewriter?'

Sitting in the back seat beside Maud, she almost cringed as the anticipated questions leapt about in her mind. They would tell Lance exactly why she was at Golden Hills, and the situation would also involve Nell, who had arranged for her to stay with them.

The remainder of the journey to Westshore was filled with deep foreboding for Janie, but strangely, when they stopped outside the house on the seafront, the situation was averted by the postman's late arrival on that particular day. Laura Meredith, who had been outside waiting for them, was in the act of taking a bundle of mail from his hand.

Janie snatched at the opportunity to say, 'I'll relieve Mother of that mail. Some of it will be magazines that are posted to me.' She left the car and hurried towards the drive entrance, where she kissed her mother, whispering in her ear as she did so, 'Please, Mother—not a word about the interview with Lance. I've decided against it.'

Laura looked at her blankly. 'But why, dear?'

'I'll explain *later*. Please don't mention the subject.'

'Very well, if you say so.' Laura was obviously puzzled.

'I do—quite definitely. Now, come and meet Lance.'

Laura looked at her quickly, but Janie avoided her mother's searching eyes.

A few minutes later, the introduction had been made and Laura and Nell had embraced each other. The Volvo left the Westshore suburb and, after passing the port where ships lay at anchor, Lance drove to a seafront restaurant on the Napier Parade.

The lunch hour was spent in pleasant but quiet chatter, steered in a subtle manner by Laura. And, despite the fact that Nell was obviously keen to talk about earlier days when they enjoyed picnic lunches at polo matches, these reminiscences were deftly substituted for topics that included Lance.

Janie smiled inwardly as she noted Laura's manoeuvring of the conversation. She knew her mother longed to talk about the old days with Nell and Maud, yet she was also endeavouring to learn a little about Lance. As the subjects were steered towards his interests, with Laura speaking knowledgeably about the current farming season, Janie longed to shout at her, 'You can save yourself the trouble, Mother. He's not even remotely interested in me. The moment we reach home he'll be rushing along the road to see *Penelope*.'

After lunch, this thought became even more firmly fixed in her mind, driven home by an unexpected request from Lance. As the three older women walked ahead, making their way towards the shops, he paused to lay a hand upon Janie's arm. 'I want you to help me choose some perfume,' he said in a low voice.

'Oh? Very well.' It was an effort to keep her voice light. Of course, it was for Penelope, she decided as a wave of misery dampened her spirits.

'It's confidential. You mustn't mention it to either Nell or Maud.' The ring in his voice confirmed that it was a command.

The shop they entered offered rows of perfumes, and within a short time Janie had selected one that met with his approval.

Lance pocketed the small gift-wrapped parcel, then turned to her with a serious expression on his handsome face. His eyes searched hers anxiously as he said, 'Now I have another request. I want you to examine the contents of the window next door. I need your opinion.'

His words were in the nature of another command, and she searched her mind, trying to recall what type of shop was situated next door. But as they approached it she was drawn to a standstill. 'It's a jeweller's shop!' she exclaimed.

'That's right.' He grinned nonchalantly.

She was not amused. 'Why should I look in a jeweller's window?'

He took her arm and drew her closer to the dazzling display of diamond rings. 'Because I'd like to have your opinion—as I've already stated. Now, tell me—which do you consider to be the most popular type of ring these days?' he asked lightly.

'Most women have their own personal choice,' she pointed out.

He waved a hand towards the window. 'So, out of an array like that—what would be *your* choice?'

She looked at him uncertainly, trying to fathom the reason for his question. Surely he wouldn't have the nerve, the utter temerity, to ask her to choose a ring for—for somebody else. The thought made her feel weak at the knees, then, before she could stop the words, she snapped furiously, 'I suppose it's for *Penelope*.'

His eyes questioned her. 'It bugs you to think so?'

'No, not at all,' she said, knowing she was lying. Of course it bugged her! Her blood ran cold as, deep down, the thought wrenched at every nerve she possessed. It made her want to scream and scream until she threw up—and it was during those few moments she knew she loved him. Yes, beyond all doubt she loved him, and the knowledge was like a bang on the back from a sledgehammer—a bang that knocked her flat. Yet she was being asked for her opinion about rings—not for herself, but for Penelope.

His voice seemed to come from a great distance, repeating the request. 'Perhaps you could give me your opinion. After all, it's all I'm asking.'

Her eyes blurred as she stared at the glitter in the window, but she managed to regain control of her emotions. Despite the difficulty, she made an effort to concentrate on the various types of rings, each one nestling in its velvet-lined box.

Eventually her voice was cool and steady as she said, 'That one, centre stage, looks like the Rock of Gibraltar. It also costs the earth.'

'You like that one?'

'Certainly not! It's far too opulent, but no doubt it would suit——'

He cut in, 'What about that bar of five diamonds?'

'Still too showy. I much prefer the cluster beneath it on the next shelf. Now, that's a beauty. I—I feel sure Penelope would love it,' she added with a touch of dejection.

'You do? Personally I think her preference would lie with the Rock of Gibraltar.'

She turned bleak eyes upon him. 'Do you intend to buy it now?' It was difficult to keep the bitterness from her voice as she visualised him slipping it on Penelope's slim finger.

The corners of his mouth twitched. 'I'll wait before

rushing into that particular purchase. Thank you for helping me decide upon the—the type of rings that girls like these days——'

'I can't see that I've done that exactly.'

'You've given me more assistance than you realise.' He glanced at his watch. 'It's almost time for the appointment with my accountant, but when I've finished with him I'll search for you in the main shopping area.'

'We'll be easy to find,' she assured him in a dull voice.

He looked at her sharply. 'Are you OK? You've gone quite pale.'

'Of course I'm all right.' Impatience with herself made her speak crossly.

'Very well, I'll see you later.'

She watched him stride away, threading between people walking along the footpath, and it was only moments before he was lost among them. She then made her way towards a wooden seat, where she sank down to think—and to control her inner turmoil of emotions, which had her perilously close to tears.

There were also her future plans to be considered, and she knew that if she had any sense at all she'd leave Golden Hills at once. But in the mean time she had to return to collect her clothes and her car, and she also knew that Nell would be hurt if she left too abruptly. But—loving Lance as she did—how long would it be possible for her to remain under the same roof and not allow him to become aware of her feelings for him?

Suddenly she sat up and straightened her back. You're being a fool to let him get into your blood, she told herself fiercely. How could you possibly fall in love with him when you've known him only since last Monday? A schoolgirl crush—that's all it is. OK, so he's a gorgeous hunk of a male and you're infatuated. The sooner you snap out of it, the better.

Although she hammered these points at herself, she was not entirely convinced. Nobody had ever affected her in this manner. No man had ever stirred this hungry longing to be with him, and she feared that, instead of waning until it entirely disappeared, it was likely to become even more intense.

Eventually she left the seat and went in search of her mother, Nell and Maud. They weren't difficult to find, because Janie automatically headed for the wool department of one of the city's larger stores. She smiled as she saw them, their attentions entirely taken up by browsing through books of knitting patterns.

Laura turned and caught sight of her. 'Ah, there you are, dear! I was beginning to wonder where you were.'

'I suppose you could call it window-shopping,' Janie said, conscious of an inner ache.

Nell said, 'Will you look at Maud—she's just bought two books of Fair-Isle caps, and she has several at home.'

'But the patterns are different and you know I love making Fair-Isle caps,' Maud reminded her.

Nell turned a protesting face to Laura. 'Would you believe she has a whole carton of Fair-Isle caps? They're beautifully made, but she just gives them away.'

'Why don't you sell them?' Laura asked briskly, the question betraying her practical nature.

'Now that's what I call common sense,' Nell exclaimed.

Maud looked blankly from one to the other. 'Sell them? Where on earth could I sell them? I mean, living out in the country——'

Laura looked at her in silence for several moments before she said, 'You could send them to Napier. Would you believe there's a shop that takes every homespun, hand-knitted item I can produce? Caps, scarves, mittens, stoles and jerseys are all sold to tourists. The shop is always short of caps. The owner is a friend of mine, and I think it's high time you met her.'

An excited giggle escaped Nell. 'Maud, dear—I believe you're about to go into business!'

Laura turned to Nell. 'You'll be able to join her.'

'But I don't need the money,' Nell protested.

'Then you can give it to your favourite charity,' Laura explained. 'That's what I do, and it gives me a feeling of intense satisfaction when I hand a cheque to Save The Children Fund, or to some other charity. Besides, it's the very thing you need, a real purpose for all that spinning and knitting. Now, come and meet my friend.'

She guided them towards a shop that specialised in souvenirs and handcrafts of all types. The woman who came forward to greet her was introduced to Nell and Maud and, when told of the reason for their visit, declared herself to be desperate for Fair-Isle caps. Her jaw dropped slightly, when Maud promised to put a carton of caps in the post on Monday. Arrangements were then made, and by the time they left the shop Nell and Maud were smiling with an excitement they were unable to conceal.

When Lance found them a short time later, they were still bubbling inwardly, their obvious exhilaration causing his brows to rise. 'Have you girls been on the bottle?' he demanded.

Laura laughed. 'Indeed they have not. But it's high time they had a cup of tea. Let's go home to Westshore, and they'll tell you about their new business project.'

He was astounded. '*Business*——? This, I must hear. Let's go.'

When they reached the seafront house, Janie became busy helping her mother with the afternoon tea, and as she carried the tray of cups and saucers out to the porch table she heard Maud explaining the arrangements to Lance.

He nodded approval. 'It's an excellent idea.'

Nell spoke eagerly. 'Indirectly, it's really Janie we have to thank, because if she hadn't been with us Laura wouldn't have been there to take us to meet her friend.'

Janie sent him a quick glance, but his eyes became veiled, almost as if he were unwilling to look at her. 'You're exaggerating, Nell,' she said lightly.

Later, when Janie had packed an extra suitcase of clothes and they were on the verge of leaving, Laura said, 'Did you see the mail I left on your bedside table, dear? There were several letters, and that sports magazine came the day after you'd left. It might have one of your——' She fell silent, possibly surprised by the agonised look flashed at her.

'Yes, they're in my bag,' Janie said.

'What sports magazine is this?' Lance drawled.

'Oh, it's just one I happen to subscribe to,' Janie answered evasively.

'I'd like to see it.'

'Later, perhaps——' She bit her lower lip thoughtfully, realising she'd be wiser to leave the magazine at home. But a quick glance had shown one of her articles to be in it, and the temptation to see it in print had been too great, therefore she'd put it in the suitcase. Also, to leave it at home now would be difficult, because the case was already outside the door, and to reopen it to extract the magazine would probably place it right into Lance's hands.

Nell said quickly, 'You haven't time to browse through magazines just now, Lance. We've a long drive ahead of us.' She turned to Laura. 'My dear, it's been so nice to see you again—and I feel really excited about our wool project. You're right when you say our spinning will take on a new meaning.' She continued to chat volubly as she prepared to leave, and the subject of the sports magazine was dropped.

But was it forgotten? Janie wondered. She noticed that Lance had little to say during the drive home, nor were there any moments when he caught and held her gaze in the rear-view mirror. His brow seemed to have taken on a permanent frown, and he appeared to have become remote. She sought in her mind for a reason, but it eluded her.

However, the journey home was anything but silent, because Nell and Maud held an animated conversation about their future plans with wool. A cool breeze blew in the partly open window beside Nell, stirring her grey hair as she chatted happily and began to count their blessings.

Her cheeks became slightly flushed as she turned to look at Maud. 'We're most *fortunate* that shearing is about to begin. We'll go to the woolshed and choose the *best* fleece——'

Maud looked at her critically. 'Nell, dear, I'm wondering if the breeze from that window is a little cool for you. You know you're inclined to catch a chill rather easily.'

But Nell ignored the hint to wind up the window. Instead, she turned to Lance with queries about the number of black sheep in the flock. 'I know that very few are actually black,' she added. 'It's the various shades of grey that we need, and of course some white wool as well——' Her words ended as a small bout of coughing shook her petite frame.

Lance sent her a sharp glance, then issued an order. 'Wind up that window immediately—otherwise you'll not get a skerrick of wool.'

Nell obeyed meekly, but not before a couple of sneezes escaped her.

However, the chatter continued, and their spirits were still high when they reached home. As they prepared the evening meal, the elated conversation between Nell and Maud floated from the kitchen.

Lance watched them from the living-room area, then spoke to Janie in a low voice. 'You appear to have given them a new lease of life and for that I'm grateful.'

She shook her head. 'Don't thank me—thank my mother. It was she who made the arrangements.'

'No doubt. But it's as Nell said—if you hadn't been with us, it wouldn't have happened.'

Grim lines had appeared about his mouth, and she was startled by the sight of them. 'Something about that fact annoys you?' she asked hesitantly.

'It's a phenomenon which still has me puzzled.' The words were clipped and coldly abrupt.

She looked at him steadily. 'You sound as if you're mad with me for some reason.'

His jaw tightened. 'I didn't say so.'

'You don't have to. Your tone makes it plain something's bugging you. What is it, exactly?'

He remained silent, staring at her from beneath lowered brows.

Her chin rose as she glared at him. 'If my presence offends you, please don't hesitate to let it be known. I'll go home immediately.'

'I've not said I want you to leave. In any case, you're now officially on the payroll—therefore, I shall require a fortnight's notice if you decide to give up the job of exercising the polo ponies.'

'I hadn't thought of doing so,' she informed him quietly. 'It's just that I can sense a change in your attitude towards me, and I can't help wondering about it.'

The expression about his mouth became sardonic. 'It really surprises you?'

'Of course it surprises me, especially after——' A hot flush stole into her cheeks as she turned away, embarrassed.

'Especially after the frolic in the hayloft, when you were leading me along so nicely. Did you have a special goal in mind?' His eyes glittered as they watched her from behind narrowed lids.

'I don't know what you're talking about!' she snapped.

'Very well—we'll leave the subject for the moment.'

The entrance of Maud, with a casserole she'd prepared before leaving that morning, put an end to further discussion. But when the lid was lifted from the savoury dish of meat and vegetables, Janie found herself unable to enjoy the meal. The thought of Lance's thinly veiled contempt caused her to have difficulty in swallowing the food which seemed to go round and round in her mouth, and it was only when she noticed Maud watching her that she pulled herself together.

'You're feeling tired,' Maud observed.

'Yes, a little,' Janie admitted. *Tired?* She felt more than tired. She was washed out—completely drained. The discovery of her love for Lance had been a shock—and to have it followed by his anger towards herself was almost unbearable.

Nell yawned. 'I shall go to bed early. A day in Napier always makes me feel weary. Are you feeling tired, Maud?'

Maud smiled happily. 'Yes, but not too tired to pack that carton of knitted caps in readiness for the post on Monday.' She turned to Lance, asking delicately, 'I suppose you'll be going visiting—as usual?'

He shrugged, then fixed her with a cool glare. 'I haven't decided. Is there some reason why I shouldn't do so?'

'No—no, of course not,' she replied hurriedly.

'Janie has lots of letters to read,' Nell said.

'At least half a dozen,' Janie confirmed. 'I shall read them in bed,' she added, knowing it would be a relief to be alone.

Lance's voice struck her ears. 'She has magazines as well,' he put in quietly.

Maud was interested. 'Which magazines do you have sent to you? Are there any with knitting patterns?'

She shook her head. 'No, they're mainly writer magazines. One comes from America, and the other is an

Australian-New Zealand publication. No knitting patterns, I'm afraid.'

'Not even in the *other* magazine?' Lance put in softly. 'I mean the one that covers various sports.' His eyes had become mocking.

'No, not even in that one,' she agreed calmly, her spirits sinking to a lower ebb, as the reason for his attitude towards her became clear in her mind. That dratted sports magazine had jogged his memory, and she felt sure he now knew that she was the one who had phoned for an interview. But, despite his refusal, she had wormed her way into his house. No wonder he was mad at her, she thought bitterly.

CHAPTER SEVEN

WHEN the meal was finished, Lance left the table abruptly. He muttered something about spending time in his office before going out, then strode from the room, his expression bleak.

Janie sensed his animosity towards herself, and as she helped Maud to clear the dishes she found difficulty in maintaining a cheerful face. She longed for the privacy of her room, and at last she made her mail and magazines the excuse for going to bed, and said goodnight.

As she passed through the hall, she saw Lance at the door opening into the garage and, determined to be affable, she said, 'Have a happy evening. I hope you haven't forgotten the perfume for Penelope.'

He turned to scowl at her. 'For your information, that perfume wasn't purchased for Penelope.'

'Oh?' Her startled tone betrayed surprise.

'No. I bought it for Maud, as a small token of appreciation for all the help she gives to Nell.'

His words cheered her slightly, although she still sensed an underlying antagonism. Words evading her, she went upstairs to prepare for bed.

She was in her flimsy nightdress when a knock sounded on the balcony door. A sharp breath escaped her. She knew it could only be Lance, and that she had no option but to open the door, therefore she slipped her arms into a wrap and tied the belt.

Opening the door, she said, 'I thought you were going to visit Penelope. Did you change your mind?'

He strode into the room. 'It's possible. As a matter of fact, I've been doing some clerical work. There are figures my accountant needs, and I've been getting them together. I should have taken them with me this morning.'

She waited in silence for him to tell her the real purpose of his visit, but he merely stared at her without speaking. At last she said, 'You came here to tell me you'd been doing office work?'

'Indeed I did not!' he almost lashed at her. 'Nor is it the only adding up I've been doing.'

'Oh?' She quailed beneath his glare.

'Why didn't you tell me who you were from the beginning?'

Her eyes widened. 'What do you mean? Are you asccusing me of trying to hide my identity?'

'You could put it that way—and you do know what I mean.' The words were clipped.

She certainly knew what he meant, but she hedged, 'That's quite ridiculous! I was introduced to you as Janine Meredith—and that's exactly who I am.'

'That—and more,' he snarled. 'When you first arrived, I couldn't remember where I'd heard the name, but now I know you're the person who rang for an interview.'

She looked at him, searching for words.

'Didn't I tell you to go hopping sideways?'

'I recall you were very rude,' she retorted coldly.

'Yet you used your mother's acquaintance with my aunt to crawl into the house.' His tone had become scathing.

'*Crawl?* How dare you——' She almost felt the colour drain from her face. 'Never in my life have I *crawled*. It wasn't like that at all.' Or was it? she wondered, trying to be honest with herself.

'No? It seems mighty like it to me. You couldn't come in the front door openly, so you sneaked in the back door—or was it the *stable* door?' he suggested, his lip curling with derision.

'Why don't you let me explain?'

'Because I'm not interested in any of the stories you're

capable of plucking out of the air.'

'Please, you're quite wrong——'

'Wrong, am I? Then let's see how far off the beam I am. You *did* phone me for an interview?'

'Yes, I did—but that was before I got here.'

'*Naturally* it was before you got here!' His lips curled again as though scorning her utter stupidity.

'After I arrived, I changed my mind.'

'Oh, yes? A likely story, I must say. What changed your mind—if it's not too much to ask?'

'I—I decided I didn't want to do the story.'

He sent her a cold glare. 'Are you saying you decided I wasn't worth the effort, after all?'

She snatched at the excuse. 'Something like that.'

'Thank you—thank you very much,' he gritted. 'Well, where's the magazine? I might as well take a look at your style of writing.'

'Why?'

'Curiosity, perhaps.' He looked about the room, then strode to the dressing-table where her mail lay waiting to be read. The magazine in question was all too obvious from its cover, and as he flicked through the pages he surprised her by saying, 'I've already seen several issues of this magazine. Penelope's father has it posted to him.'

She could only look at him wordlessly.

'When she met you last Tuesday, your name rang a bell, and before she left she remembered where she'd seen it. Of course, it was in this magazine.'

'And so she told you about it.'

'Penelope knew I'd been asked for an interview, and she also knew I'd refused. She's well aware that I *never* give interviews. When she recognised your name, she warned me that you'd got yourself into the house to do *just that*. When I said I didn't believe her, she told me she could show me your name in various issues of the magazine. I must say I was shocked—and bitterly disappointed in you.'

'Now I know why you were so cool to me after your sessions with Penelope.' The weeping inside her was increasing steadily, and in an effort to control it she tried to ignore his obvious contempt, and said, 'I can't help wondering why you're so against being interviewed. Is there a reason that makes you so adamant?'

'Of course there's a reason—and a very simple reason, for that matter. It's because I don't trust reporters. So many of them are inclined to twist the truth—put things out of content—leave out the true facts in favour of sensation——'

'Are you saying you've had experience of this sort?'

'Yes. It was after my father's death. The reports of it sounded as though he'd committed suicide. It was most distressing to Nell and to me, and since then I've distrusted reporters of any description. I promised myself I'd *never* give an interview.'

Her chin rose as she glared at him. 'You've no right to suggest that I'd write in that manner! Surely you can give me credit for a little integrity?'

He gave a scornful laugh. '*Integrity?* After the way in which you've wangled yourself into this house? You've got to be joking.'

His words made her tremble. Her lip quivered and her eyes widened until they were two dark blue daubs in a white face. She racked her brains for excuses that would exonerate herself, but her mind seemed to have gone blank.

It was then that he noticed her cassette recorder on the bedside table. A few strides took him to it and, lifting it, he snarled, 'Well, well—what have we here? A neat Japanese Sanyo with built-in speaker. Just the job to record the unguarded words of a poor fool—an idiot who allows himself to be interviewed by a smart cookie who rewrites the results in a manner to raise eyebrows.'

The accusation aimed at herself was enough to loosen a storm of fury. 'You listen to me!' she shouted, almost choking over the words. 'It's time you heard my side of the story. It's true that the editor of the magazine asked me to interview you, and when I told him you'd refused he asked me to try again——'

'And again—and again——' he sneered, his voice dripping with sarcasm.

She ignored the interruption. 'Mother spoke to Nell about it, and between them they decided that—quite apart from any interview—I'd be a suitable person to take over Peter Bryant's job of exercising the polo ponies.' She paused to draw a deep breath, then hissed, 'Is that clear enough to you?'

'Quite clear. I wondered how Nell came to have a hand in it.'

'Please understand, she was only trying to help you. Well, I'd been here only a few hours when I scrapped all plans for doing the interview.'

'Why?' The question was snapped at her.

'I felt I was here under false pretences.'

'Ah! You admit that much.'

'Of course. It niggled and irritated me, because it was against my principles. I told Nell that I'd put the idea out of my head and that I'd just concentrate on exercising the ponies.'

He looked at her closely. 'The ponies mean so much to you?'

It was her turn to be scornful. 'Surely you don't have to be overbright to understand that the ponies are giving me back part of my old life. I suppose you could say I've been reaching out to clutch at the past, and at a time that was so very dear to me. However, that's all over now—and I'm afraid you'll have to find somebody else to work the horses.'

'What do you mean?'

'I mean that, if you'll leave this room, I'll dress and pack my other bag.'

'You're forgetting I need a period of notice,' he scowled.

'Two weeks, to be exact.'

'You can whistle for it,' she flashed at him. 'I have no intention of working for a man who holds me in contempt.' She bent swiftly and dragged her suitcase from beneath the bed.

His scowl became even darker. 'You really mean you'll leave in the morning?'

'No, I mean I'll leave *tonight*—immediately!' she snapped. 'As soon as I'm dressed and packed, I'll be on my way. I'll tell Nell that I know exactly what you think of me, and any further explanation to her will be up to you.'

'She'll be most upset.'

'I'm aware of that.'

'She'll also be thoroughly disappointed in *you*.'

'For not staying to help *you*. I suppose. I'm afraid it can't be helped, and she'll understand when she thinks about it.'

'It could keep her awake all night,' he warned.

'Yes, that's possible. Is there anything else?' she asked with forced politeness.

'Only that she's inclined to go down very easily. There's not a great deal of stamina in Nell's small body. Sit her in a draught and she takes a chill immediately. The shock of your unexpected departure will knock her flat. Is that something you want to do?'

'No—no, of course not.' Even as she spoke, she knew she had no wish to upset Nell, the small woman who had been so kind to her. It was Nell who had given her the opportunity to get close to the man she wished to interview, and—who knew?—it *might* have eventuated if things had worked out differently. No, she couldn't hurt Nell by leaving so abruptly.

'So what shall you do?' he rasped impatiently. 'I'd be glad if you'd make up your mind. Do you intend to go, or stay at least for tonight?' His tone had become cold.

Her face betrayed her indecision, as she tried to control the tears that were perilously near.

'Well, what is it to be?' he demanded angrily.

Her lip quivered slightly as she said, 'I'm well aware that you couldn't care less whether I stay or leave, but for Nell's sake I'll not rush out of the house tonight.'

'Then why the devil couldn't you have said so in the first instance. Really, I could shake the living daylights out of you.' His extreme exasperation was betrayed as his strong hands gripped her shoulders in a movement that almost made her bones rattle.

She gasped as the onslaught of vibration caused her already loosened belt to fall from her waist. Her gown fell open, revealing the rise of rounded breasts beneath the low neck of her nightdress, and she heard a sharp breath escape him as he stared at her.

She made a wild clutch at her gown, but he jerked it from her shoulders, causing it to fall to the floor. Twisting, she tried to turn her back on him, but firm hands spun her round to face him again. As she crossed her arms in a vain attempt to hide her breasts, she could only stare at him helplessly.

'Please, go away——' she whispered in a pathetic voice.

'Like hell!' he snapped.

A sudden movement swept her up into his arms, cradling her like a small child. For several moments he stared down into her face, his eyes holding an intangible glitter as he strode closer to the bed, where he laid her gently on the cover before stretching himself beside her.

Loving him as she did, she was powerless to do other than respond, by clinging with arms that encircled his body. The blood pounded through her veins, causing her nerves to tingle, and she knew she must control her leaping desire. But it seemed beyond her ability to do so with his hard mouth taking possession of her own in a slow yet seductive kiss that made no secret of his demands.

Leaving her mouth, his lips trailed their way to her throat, giving her the opportunity to murmur a protesting, 'No, Lance—please stop. Why are you doing this to me?'

'Isn't it obvious?' His muttered words floated up to her ears. 'You're not a child, Janie. You're a woman, and one of the most desirable I've ever met.'

'You surprise me. A few moments ago I could have sworn you positively hated me.'

'Hated you?' He gave a low chuckle. 'That'll be the day.'

'But you don't trust me,' she persisted. 'You consider me to be a—a deceiving little——' The words ended in a gasp as a vulnerable nerve in her neck received his attention, causing her arms to clasp him even more tightly.

As she held him closely, she listened for the words that would tell her he *did* trust her, but he didn't speak. Instead, his lips made their way down to her breast. They nuzzled gently at a taut rosebud, and as they did so his hand slipped beneath her nightdress to knead the muscles of her back, then moved with feather-softness up and down her spine.

She felt the gentleness of his touch move to the firm flatness of her stomach, and as her flesh was set on fire faint little moans escaped her, mingling with the blurred warnings that struggled to reach her brain. Her hands moved to push him away but, instead of using strength against him, her fingers became entangled in his thick dark hair, while she lapped up the joy of these precious moments of being held in his arms.

Suddenly they came to an end. The electricity between them was switched off abruptly, as sounds in the passage caused them to freeze. Nell and Maud had come up the stairs, and Maud's voice came clearly to their ears.

'You get into bed, dear,' she said to Nell. 'I'll bring you a nice hot drink of Horlicks and you'll feel better in the morning. You've had a long day and you're overtired.' Her voice faded as she moved away.

Janie struggled from Lance's arms, as she sat up with a jerk. 'Please, you must go,' she whispered tremulously.

'You're right,' he agreed gruffly, leaving the bed and then vanishing through the balcony door.

Dazed, she stared at the place he'd left, trying to believe he'd actually been beside her, but only the dent made by the weight of his body remained and the rest seemed like a dream.

Moments later, a tap on the door was followed by the sound of Maud's voice. 'Are you still awake, Janie?'

She slipped between the sheets and dragged the blankets beneath her chin. 'Yes, come in——'

Maud's head came round the door. 'I'll be bringing a hot drink to Nell. Would you like one, too? It's Horlicks.'

A hot drink would soothe her nerves and help her to sleep, she thought. 'Yes, thank you—I'd love a hot drink, but I'll come down and get it. You don't have to wait on me.'

'Nonsense, you'll stay there. It just means another cup on the tray I'll bring up to Nell. She's complaining of a sore throat, so I thought she'd be wise to go to bed. I hope it's not the beginning of a nasty cold for her.' And before further protest could come from Janie, Maud disappeared.

For a moment she lay against the pillows, relieved at not having to go downstairs. She still felt shaken by the intensity of her own surging emotions, and she knew that Lance had been on fire with the desire to make love—yet there had been no actual words of love, no commitment of any sort. But, of course, there wouldn't be.

The memory of his hands on her body made her feel hot, and she knew she should be thankful for the timely interruption Nell and Maud had provided. She also knew that an effort must be made to control her thoughts and, springing out of bed, she snatched up her letters and the magazine.

Most of the letters were from schoolfriends with whom she'd kept in touch, and she was in the midst of reading them when Maud returned.

'I don't like the look of Nell,' the older woman said anxiously. 'Her face is very flushed, and her voice has become quite husky. I can't help feeling I should have noticed that open car window much sooner than I did.'

'Nell's not a child,' Janie pointed out. 'Shouldn't she have noticed the draught? I can't see that you should be blaming yourself?'

But it was plain that Maud *did* blame herself, and the worried frown was still clouding her brow when she left the room to return to Nell.

Janie then turned to the sports magazine which carried an article she'd written about the Ruapehu ski fields in the centre of the North Island. The photos she'd taken had come up well, and as usual the words she'd strung together looked better when seen on the printed page. She felt mildly satisfied with her efforts.

The magazine itself was not large and glossy; instead, it was an unpretentious publication which covered sports of all descriptions. Holding it in her hand, she gazed at it almost unseeingly as she realised it had affected her life. It had caused her to come to Golden Hills, and through it she had met Lance. Now it was to be the cause of her break with him.

Despite the recent magic moments on the bed, she knew she would be wise to leave in the morning. He had been ready and willing to take all she had to offer, yet—obviously—had nothing to give in return. Making love with him had been so *near*, and she knew she must get out while she was still in one piece and before she completely lost her head. And with this decision made, she slept.

But she had reckoned without Nell. When morning came, the small woman was forced to stay in bed. Her face was even more flushed, her head throbbed and her body ached.

Maud was much more concerned about her. 'She's got a dose of the 'flu,' she informed Janie when she came down to breakfast. 'My goodness, am I thankful to have you here! The poor dear becomes so upset when she thinks I have too much extra to do—like running up and down the stairs with meals.'

'Don't worry, I'll help,' Janie assured her, knowing it meant she'd be unable to leave Golden Hills as quickly as she had intended.

Secretly she was pleased to have the excuse to stay. She was also conscious of an immense feeling of relief, because she could now remain without Lance wondering about the question of what had prompted her to extend her visit when she'd been so adamant about leaving. It would be ghastly if he suspected she was staying because of *him*. 'Can I take breakfast up to Nell?' she offered.

Maud shook her head. 'She says she doesn't want anything—not even a cup of tea—and I can assure you there's something wrong when Nell doesn't want her cup of tea. Perhaps the aspirins I've given her will help to ease the aches and pains, and I'm also giving her lemon and honey.'

Janie hurried through her breakfast, then hastened upstairs to peep into Nell's room. The small woman appeared to be asleep, so she left quietly and made her way downstairs and out towards the stable. The horses were already in the yard, and as she drew near she could see that Lance was putting the saddle on Major.

He paused as she approached, stared at her without speaking, then went to the stable for the second saddle. As he placed it on Gay's back, he said nonchalantly, 'I was sure you'd be half-way to Napier by this time.'

'Nell's got the 'flu. Didn't Maud tell you? I'm not leaving while she's sick.'

'No?' He became busy with Gay's girth and surcingle.

'Maud seems to be glad I'm here.'

'That's easily understood.'

'I felt I couldn't leave when I might be able to help in some small way like—like carrying a tray upstairs—or by trying to cheer Nell if she becomes lonely up in her room while Maud's busy downstairs.' Her tongue seemed to be rattling on aimlessly, as she sought for face-saving reasons that enabled her to remain at Golden Hills.

'Then I'll count myself fortunate you'll continue to exercise the ponies—at least in the mean time.' His grin was sardonic as he handed Gay's rein to her.

Not a word about last night, she noticed, as she took a discreet peep at the handsome face. At the same time, she detected a cool remoteness in his attitude towards her, a definite aloofness that made her wonder if he'd deliberately washed those moments on the bed from his mind.

And this seemed to be the case when he said, 'The tide's right out. We'll take them down to the sands.' The words, clipped and brief, were followed by a silence.

They led the horses past the stable and beyond the pine plantations where breezes sighed in the branches overhead. In an effort to make amicable conversation, Janie said, 'Just look at those pine cones lying on the ground. They'd be wonderful on the open fire.'

'They are. The men gather them by the sackful.' His tone was still abrupt.

Looking over her shoulder, she remarked brightly, 'Some of them are really large—the largest I've ever seen, I think.'

'And surprisingly heavy when they fall,' he said gruffly.

There was another long silence, until they had gone through the gate and were on the beach, and by that time Janie was becoming irritated by his belligerent manner. Forcing a smile to her lips, she turned to him and said, 'Would you prefer to ride alone?'

He sent her a sharp glance. 'Of course not. Why do you ask?'

'Because you appear to be engrossed in morbid thoughts of your own—or else you're sulking.'

'I never sulk,' he snapped.

'No? You could have fooled me!'

'I'll admit that I'm annoyed——'

'With me, of course. I quite understand, but I have tried to explain that I'd dropped all idea of an interview.'

'You're wrong. I'm more annoyed with myself than with you.'

She turned surprised eyes upon him. 'Why should you be annoyed with yourself?'

'For my lack of control last night.'

A deep flush stole into her cheeks. 'I presume you mean—on the bed. You're saying you regret we were—so close? OK——' she flared angrily. 'All you have to do is— *forget it*!'

'I'm afraid I can't.'

Nor could she herself forget it, but she dared not say so. Instead she said, 'I suppose it makes you feel guilty—I mean, because of your association with Penelope.'

'Don't be stupid!' he gritted.

And then the sight of a distant figure on horseback brought an exclamation from her. 'Isn't that Penelope, riding along the water's edge?'

'Yes. She often takes morning rides on the sands.'

'You arranged to meet her here? I'm sorry if I've barged in. I've no wish to intrude, so I'll leave you alone together. Perhaps you'll feel better after you've made a confession to her,' she added as an afterthought.'

'Will you please stop making idiotic statements?' he rasped.

As Penelope came cantering towards them, Janie saw that her long dark hair had been left loose to blow in the wind. Her cheeks were glowing and her eyes sparkled like jet, making her look like an attractive gypsy.

'Hi there, I was hoping to see you,' she called gaily to Lance.

Janie sent her a bright smile. 'Good morning, Penelope.'

But the greeting went unanswered, as Penelope ranged

her horse beside Major and began an animated conversation with Lance. 'That new horse has arrived,' she told him. 'I mean, the one that's to replace Sam's Tinker. You promised to examine it before I buy it.'

He nodded. 'I'll drive over this afternoon.'

'Thank you, that'll be lovely.' Penelope flashed a dazzling smile at him. 'Perhaps you could bring Nell with you. It's time she came to see Mother, and it will also give her the chance to get away from Maud for a short time.'

Lance's brows rose. 'Is it necessary for her to do that?'

'Of course it is,' Penelope assured him. 'She never seems to go anywhere without Maud. Everybody needs a change, and I do think that Maud dominates her.'

Janie felt compelled to spring to Maud's defence. 'I think Maud *supports*, rather than *dominates* Nell,' she said quietly.

Penelope sent her a cold glare. 'Did somebody ask for your opinion, Janine Meredith?'

'No, but I'm giving it just the same,' Janie retorted. 'Nell's very fond of Maud. She relies on her implicitly. The usual employer-housekeeper relationship has been replaced by real friendship.'

Penelope tossed her hair back from her face. 'Nevertheless, she's still a servant, and my mother is *not* in the habit of entertaining other people's *servants*.'

'That sort of snobbery makes me sick!' Janie snaped furiously. 'I find that type of attitude quite insufferable. Don't you know that the days of real servants are over in this country?'

'Not as far as I'm concerned,' Penelope retorted icily. She turned to Lance. 'You will bring Nell—*alone*—this afternoon?'

'I'm afraid that's highly unlikely.' The exchange between Janie and Penelope had brought an amused expression to his face.

'Are you saying she'd refuse to come without Maud?' Penelope demanded incredulously.'

'That's more than possible, but as it happens she won't be visiting anyone this afternoon. She's in bed with 'flu, and likely to remain there for several days.'

'Oh, poor Nell—*poor little Nell!*' Penelope gushed, making a vain effort to make her sympathy sound sincere. 'When did she become ill?'

'Last night, I think,' Lance said, then added drily, 'But don't worry—she's in Maud's capable hands.'

'Oh, but I *do* worry about her,' Penelope declared, her attitude changing suddenly as she added, 'And *poor Maud*— she'll be run off her feet, going up and down those stairs to attend to Nell.'

'I intend to help her,' Janie put in quickly.

Penelope swept her with a scornful glance. '*You?* And what about the ponies, may I ask? Aren't you supposed to be exercising them? You can't be doing all the things that Nell will need, and be out on the hills at the same time.'

'You're forgetting I'm there at meal times,' Janie reminded her. 'I'll carry her trays up for Maud.'

'Her *trays,*' Penelope sneered. 'Do you imagine that's enough? Maud will need help all the time, and Nell will need more attention than Maud can give her. She'll need to be sponged . . . and—and helped to the toilet——'

Lance frowned. 'You make her sound as though she's on her last legs. I assure you she'll be OK in a few days.'

'Only if she's looked after *properly.*' Penelope persisted. 'I'd better come and help,' she added with determination.

Janie heard the last words with dismay. She glanced at Lance and saw that he was still frowning, but felt relief when he shook his head. 'You're exaggerating the whole situation,' she heard him tell Penelope.

'It could be more serious than you realise,' she warned.

'Yes, definitely—they need my help. And you need Janine's help with the ponies, therefore she can't be taken away from them. Am I right?'

'Yes, I suppose so,' he admitted gloomily.

'You still have a spare bedroom, I think.' Her voice was full of purpose.

'Yes. Why do you ask?' He eyed her suspiciously.

'Because I intend to return with you this afternoon. I'll settle into it and stay until Nell has recovered. In the mean time, I'll go home and pack a bag.' She jerked the reins and set off at a canter, before Lance could utter a word of protest.

Janie stole glances at him as they moved along the beach. His face was expresionless as he stared straight ahead, and she wondered what he felt about the prospect of having Penelope living in the house. As for herself—the mere thought of it had sent her spirits plunging down to the tide marks on the beach.

Forcing a smile, she said, 'Penelope's a very determined woman.'

'Maud is also a determined woman. I'm not sure she'll want help from Penelope. In fact, I'm not sure they can live in the same house for any length of time,' he added reluctantly.

'I doubt that it'll be for long,' Janie said, more from wishful thinking than knowledge.

'It's an experiment that'll be interesting to watch,' he mused.

She looked at him thoughtfully. 'Are you saying it could be an experiment that'll guide your future plans?'

He turned to frown at her. 'What do you mean by my future plans? Are you thinking of something? Please be frank. I like people to be honest,' he added drily.

The hint that he considered her to have been anything but honest with him sent red flags into her cheeks, and it also decided her to tell him exactly what she thought. 'Very well. I—I presume you intend to marry Penelope?'

'Who says so?' he demanded curtly.

She gave a slight shrug. 'I believe it's generally assumed, therefore I can understand that a period with her in the house will help you decide what to do about Nell and Maud when you're married.' She paused, wondering if this meant divulging a confidence, then took the plunge. 'You may not realise it, but they also have plans against the day you bring Penelope in as mistress.'

He was astounded. 'They *have*? Please enlighten me.'

'Naturally, they'll move out and live in a flat at Napier, or perhaps at Westshore. Can't you understand it's something they've had to think about?'

'I can't imagine Golden Hills without Nell. She was born here and somehow seems to be part of the place.'

'No doubt it will hurt her to leave, but in this life nothing stays the same.' Janie sighed, thinking of her own circumstances which had been changed by her father's unexpected death.

It was lunch time before they reached home, and as they sat at the table Maud informed Lance that she'd phoned the doctor in the nearest small township. 'Doctor Watts said to give her two aspirin every four hours and plenty of lemon drinks. Thank goodness the lemon tree is bowed down with fruit. I'm to ring him at once if she begins a constant coughing, or if I'm really worried about her, otherwise it will just have to run its course.'

Janie remained silent, waiting for Lance to give Maud the news concerning Penelope's arrival. He seemed to be taking a long time to do so, but at last he said, 'Well—help is on the way.'

Maud raised enquiring brows. 'Help? What do you mean?'

'We saw Penelope on the beach. When she heard about Nell's illness she said she'd come and stay for a time to give you a hand.'

Maud sat up straight as she stared directly at Lance. 'In what way would she be giving me a hand?'

'I think she intends to take over the nursing of Nell——'

'But that's ridiculous!' Maud cut in. 'I don't need her

help. It's not as though Nell is ill with pneumonia—it's only a dose of 'flu. Besides, you know as well as I do that she won't want to be attended to by Penelope. And, in any case, Janie will be here.'

'Janie will be busy with the horses,' he pointed out. 'She's unlikely to be in the house when you need her.'

Maud's manner became cold and, still sitting as though she had a ramrod down her back, she asked icily, 'Is Penelope coming to take over the household? I'd like to get this matter straight in my mind.'

Lance chuckled. 'Good heavens, no! What on earth would make you imagine such a situation?'

But Maud was not amused. 'I'm just trying to be sure of my own position here—I mean, with Penelope in the house.'

'Naturally, you're in charge,' Lance assured her. 'You'll run the house just as you always do. What you say will be law, just as it is always. There's no need to get so uptight because Pen is coming to do you a good turn.' He chuckled again.

'Just so long as I know,' Maud retorted grimly. She then turned to Janie. 'Remember, you're a witness to that statement about my word being law.'

But Janie was pondering another point. 'There's one question I can't help wondering about,' she admitted.

'You're allowed to ask,' Lance said.

'Has the patient herself no say in this matter? Suppose Nell isn't happy to have Penelope attending her? Is she to be forced into tolerating a situation she doesn't want, especially when she's sick and in a helpless position?'

'Nell will appreciate Penelope's good intentions,' he assured her complacently. 'She'll be glad to have her around.'

'We know who'll be glad to have her around,' Maud commented with barely concealed irritation. She stood up abruptly and left the room to go upstairs to Nell.

Lance appeared to ignore her remark, as well as her departure. He leaned forward and patted Janie's hand, his unexpected touch almost making her jump. 'You're looking worried, Blue-eyes. Is the situation so very bad? After all, it's only one where a neighbour is coming in to help.'

'It's more than that—and you know it. It's a situation that will upset both Maud and Nell,' she told him seriously.

Maud's remark had cut into Janie with the sharpness of a bitterly cold wind. Of course she was right—and they both knew who wanted to see Penelope in the house. It was Lance himself. If this were not so, he wouldn't be allowing Penelope to install herself in his home quite so easily.

CHAPTER EIGHT

LANCE leaned back in his chair as he regarded Janie with a hint of surprise. 'Did you expect me to throw Pen's offer back in her face?' he asked. 'She'd have been hurt.'

She looked at him steadily. 'You'd rather hurt Nell and Maud than hurt Penelope? I think that speaks for itself. You're in love with her and you want her to be here.' The accusation rushed out before she could control her tongue.

He studied her face, his eyes glinting from behind narrowed lids. 'I can see you're upset. It's written all over you. Could it possibly be because of what you think I feel for Penelope?'

The flush that had risen became deeper. 'It's because of your *lack* of feeling for Nell and Maud,' she almost hissed.

Surprisingly, he grinned. 'You're worrying unduly. You don't know Maud. You just watch her cope with the situation.'

'Do you really think she will?'

'I'm sure of it. And kindly remember that it was not I who asked Penelope to come—she just barged in of her own accord. It was entirely her own idea.'

'Yes, I suppose that's true.' Janie sighed, her despondency still weighing heavily.

His scrutiny of her face became critical. 'You look depressed. Is it possible you're taking the problems of this household too much to heart?'

She found difficulty in meeting his eyes. 'I suppose so—even if they're not my concern.'

'Then why give them so much as a second thought?'

'Because Nell and Maud are two very dear people. I don't like to see them upset, just because Penelope decides to take matters into her own hands—and—and because

133

you're happy to sit back and watch her do so,' she finished
with a rush.

'You don't hesitate to say what you think.'

'I'm only stating the truth.'

'Something tells me you don't like Penelope.'

'I don't know your—very dear friend well enough to like
or dislike her, but when you're married I—er—I wish you
joy of each other.'

In its own way, this statement reflected the truth. She
loved him deeply enough to put his happiness above her
own, and if his choice of a life partner lay with Penelope
there was nothing she could do about it.

'You're so sure we'll be married?' His words came softly.

'It seems highly probable to me.' Her eyes were filled
with more unhappiness than she realised. 'Otherwise you'd
have galloped after her this morning. You'd have pointed
out that her assistance wasn't necessary.'

'I can still do that this afternoon when I go to see Sam's
pony.'

'Oh, yes, you *could*—but I doubt that you'll do so.'

Almost choking over the last words, she left the table
abruptly and ran upstairs to see Nell. Maud was sitting
beside the small woman who looked no larger than a child
as she lay in the bed, her face still flushed and her usually
bright eyes heavily-lidded.

'How do you feel?' Janie asked with forced brightness.

Nell gave a wan smile. 'Poorly. My throat's still sore, but
the aspirins are chasing away the aches and pains.'

'Have you been coughing?' Janie asked anxiously.

'No, thank goodness. I could be a lot worse than I am, and
I'm so thankful to have my dear Maud with me.' She
paused, then asked huskily, 'Have you been riding?'

Janie nodded. 'We took the horses to the beach. Penelope
was there and we chatted for a while.' She fell silent,
lacking the courage to ask if Nell had been informed of
Penelope's plans, but an imperceptible movement of

Maud's head indicated that the patient was aware of the situation.

Nell frowned. 'Lance had arranged to meet Penelope on the beach?'

'I don't think so, otherwise he wouldn't have taken me with him.'

Nell sighed. 'No, I suppose not.' Her lips tightened, then quivered. 'Oh, dear, what shall I do? I don't want Penelope——'

'You'll do nothing,' Maud said with brisk firmness. 'Nor will you let the thought of her disturb you, because you'll be in my hands.' She stood up to adjust the pillow and straighten the bedclothes, with all the efficiency of a trained nurse.

Janie tried to add words of comfort. 'She'll be here for only a few days,' she assured Nell, with a forced brightness she was far from feeling.

But Nell was unconvinced. 'Don't you *see*?' she quavered. 'Once she's *in*—we'll never get her *out*!'

Lance's voice spoke from the doorway. He had heard the last few remarks and now gave an amused laugh. 'That's utter humbug, Nell, but we forgive these delusions when you're not well.' He turned to Janie. 'Didn't you tell them how this situation came about?'

'Are you asking if I've explained it was entirely Penelope's idea?'

'Well, wasn't it?' His glare seemed to defy her to say otherwise. 'You were there when the idea hit her.'

'Yes, but I'm sure they'd rather hear it from you.'

'After all, she's only trying to *help*. Surely you can appreciate that small fact?' His eyes went from Nell to Maud, then rested upon Janie almost accusingly for her lack of understanding.

'Of course she's coming to help,' Janie agreed smoothly. *Help herself towards more permanent residency*, her mind added silently. Then, fearing she might say something she'd regret, she moved to leave the room. 'I'll go back to the horses, if you'll excuse me.'

Moments later, she was making her way to the stable, and had almost reached it when she became aware that Lance was following her, his long strides enabling him to catch up with her rapidly.

Turning to face him, she forced a note of gaiety into her voice. 'You're going to ride? I expected to hear the Volvo tearing down the drive at high speed—small stones flying in all directions——'

His mouth twisted. 'You did? Your imagination does you credit. As it happens, I've decided to put Major and Dandy through the poles before going to see Sam's new pony.'

'And before you bring Penelope home.' Somehow the words slipped out before she could stop them.

'The thought of her arrival appears to annoy you as much as it does Nell and Maud,' he said tersely.

'Of course it doesn't,' she denied. 'Why should it?'

'Why indeed?' He removed a saddle from its rack. 'Somehow I sense that it does—if only you'd be honest.'

She evaded that particular question by saying, 'If you know that her arrival will upset both Nell and Maud, why are you allowing her to come?'

'Because I see it as an opportunity for them to learn to know her better. They're antagonistic towards her, and I'm hoping that a few days together will enable them to see she's not such a bad sort, after all. In isolated country areas, it's important for neighbours to be friends, as you yourself probably know.'

'Oh, yes—I'm well aware of that fact.'

'Penelope is also aware of it, therefore she's coming to see what she can do while Nell is sick.'

'*I'll bet she is,*' Janie agreed with more force than she'd intended. She then realised that Lance had noticed the emphasis, because his raised brows indicated his surprise. However, he made no comment, and a short time later they were riding along the farm road towards the poles.

As they followed its curves between the hills, little was

said between them until Janie fought her depression by examining and remarking upon the good condition of the rapidly growing lambs that grazed beside their mothers. At times she gazed up at flocks of birds flying overhead. Their black and white plumage interested her, and at last, in an effort to make conversation she said, 'Those are very small seagulls.'

He glanced upward. 'They're not seagulls, they're Cape pigeons. They stay around the inshore waters, scavenging for offal. Sometimes their nests can be seen on ledges along the cliffs.'

After that there was another long silence until they reached their destination, where Major and Dandy were given their pole exercises first. Lance then nodded a brief farewell to Janie, and left her to attend to Joy and Gay.

As she watched him ridng back towards the stable, a lump rose in her throat and, dismounting, she wandered across the grass to the nearby haybarn, where she tethered the two fillies to its uprights. She then stood still, to savour the memory of being held close to Lance, the recollection being so vivid she could almost hear the rain that had been falling on the roof. The faint meow of greeting that came from Cinders made those moments even more real, and as Janie swept the little black cat into her arms the tears trickled down her cheeks.

A short weep did much to relieve her feelings, and she then took Gay and Joy back to the poles, exercising each one in turn. Eventually they were given a sharp canter back to the stable, where they were unsaddled and let loose in the paddock.

It was late in the afternoon when Lance returned, and by that time the horses had been fed and Janie had changed into her jade check dress. She was busily carding wool for Maud when she heard the Volvo, and a hasty peep through the living-room door showed that the car contained only one person.

It wasn't easy to conceal her relief as she turned to Maud,

who was in the kitchen area. 'He's alone—Penelope hasn't come.'

'Thank goodness!' Maud exclaimed.

But relief was short-lived, because a few minutes later Penelope's car followed the Volvo. It stopped near the living-room door and Janie's heart sank as Penelope carried her suitcase across the veranda.

'Lance made me come in my own car,' she explained with an air of satisfaction. 'He said it would make me feel more independent, and that I could come and go as I wished. Isn't he *thoughtful*?'

Maud came forward to greet her, a broad smile of welcome lighting her features. 'Ah, there you are, Penelope—I understand you've come to give me a hand. It's *very* kind of you, and I appreciate it. There's a lot of work for one person in this big house.'

Penelope looked about her. 'It's a beautiful home. I've always loved it, even from when I was a child. Where shall I be sleeping? I hope it's the small room next to Lance.'

'No, Janie has that one,' Maud told her pleasantly. 'I've put you in the larger one, across the passage. I'm sure you'll be quite comfortable in it.'

Maud's attitude puzzled Janie. She was being so *nice*— almost as if she were delighted that Penelope had arrived. And then she smiled inwardly as Maud went on amicably, 'Before we go upstairs we'll have a little talk to discuss what's to be done—and where we stand.'

Penelope looked at her uncertainly. 'Where we stand?'

'Yes. I mean about the work.'

'Oh, you mean the work of looking after Nell.'

'Indeed I do not!' Maud's tone became indignant. 'Nell's no trouble at all. The poor dear is just lying there without a word of complaint. She's the least of the household chores.'

Penelope was startled. '*Household chores?* Surely you don't expect me to be doing——'

But Maud cut in, 'I'm preparing a little fish dish, which I hope Nell will eat—so perhaps you would get on with peeling the potatoes. They're already on the bench.'

Penelope's jaw sagged. '*Potatoes?* You've got to be joking!'

'Why should I be joking?' Maud's voice held surprise.

'You're actually expecting *me* to peel *potatoes*?'

'Of course. Aren't you here to help?' Maud's tone had now become brisk. 'Our roast is in the oven and the potatoes have to be cooked. There are carrots to be scrubbed and Brussels sprouts to be washed, after their ends have been cut criss-cross.'

'Why hasn't Janine done the potatoes?' Penelope demanded indignantly. 'She's only fiddling with that wool!'

Maud became cross. 'She is not "only fiddling", as you seem pleased to put it,' she snapped impatiently. 'She's carding it in readiness to be spun. Nell and I have an exciting new project before us.'

But Penelope was not interested in new projects. She picked up her suitcase and moved towards the hall door. 'I'll go up and see Nell,' she declared in a cold and haughty tone that was meant to put Maud in her place. 'I'll tell her I've come to take care of her—and you might as well know I have *not* come here to peel *potatoes*.'

Maud sent a glare across the room. 'Very well, Penelope. Go up and see Nell. Find out what you can do for her, and then come down and tell me. I'll be most interested.'

Penelope's expression became even more arrogant. 'I'll do that,' she snapped as she left the room.

Janie suppressed a giggle. Had Maud met her match? Bossing Nell was one thing—but bossing Penelope was something very different, she thought as she watched Maud turn towards the microwave oven.

Lance came in a few minutes later. He crossed the room to her side, and stood with his back to the flames leaping in the fireplace. 'Penelope is upstairs?' he asked.

'Yes, she's gone up to see Nell,' Janie told him, conscious of an inner flutter as she looked at the handsome face.

He stared down at her. 'I'm hoping you and Penelope

will become good friends,' he said in a low voice.

She looked up to send him a direct stare. 'Oh? Why?'

'For the reason I gave you earlier. People who live in country areas shouldn't have antagonism between them.'

'I don't live in a country area—I live at Napier's Westshore beach,' she reminded him. Then, as he merely looked at her in silence, she went on, 'Perhaps you've failed to notice that any hand of friendship I've held towards Penelope has been brushed aside. She has no wish to be friendly with me.'

He frowned. 'Why should that be?'

The reason was more than obvious to Janie, but it was not one she could discuss with him, therefore she said, 'Perhaps she considers I'm here under false pretences—just as you yourself do——'

'If I can forgive your entry through the back door, so can she.'

Surprise was reflected in the blue eyes raised to his. 'You do forgive me? Thank you.'

'Hasn't it been obvious to you? Didn't those few minutes on the bed tell you anything?'

'What were they supposed to tell me? That you wanted me to stay on for the sake of the ponies?'

A small muscle worked in his jaw as he looked at her in silence, until he asked, 'Is that what you really thought?'

She found difficulty in meeting his gaze, but at last she looked up at him, her eyes questioning. Then, through not watching what she was doing, one of the sharp pins on the carding hackle caught her finger, causing blood to ooze from the broken flesh, and bringing forth a small cry of pain.

Lance said, 'Come and wash it in the laundry.'

She fumbled for a handkerchief. 'It'll be all right——'

'Do as you're told.' The order came sharply.

She followed him obediently, and made no protest when he held her hand beneath a stream of cold water running from the tap. He then took a first-aid box from a cupboard, wiped the cut dry and dabbed it with a solution of bright red Mercurochrome.

'It's an antiseptic,' he explained, taking a duster from the box and wrapping it about her finger.

'Thank you.' She marvelled at the gentleness of his touch, but was not prepared for his unexpected movement when he carried her hand to his lips.

'There, now—that should make it better,' he said, as though speaking to a child.

'A most touching scene.' Penelope's sneering tones came from the doorway. Her dark eyes glittered angrily as they rested upon Janie, but within moments she had herself under control. 'Maud sent me to find you. She says dinner is on the table,' she added, as she took Lance's arm in a possessive manner.

Dinner was a subdued affair that evening. Maud and Penelope remained distantly polite to each other, while Janie did her best to offer cheerful conversation. Lance, sitting at the head of the table, had little to say, but appeared to be quietly assessing the attitudes the three women held towards each other.

'I understand you've been up to see Nell,' he said to Penelope.

'Naturally, I went up almost as soon as I arrived,' she told him self-righteously. 'Did you imagine I'd delay?'

'Not at all. I'm sure she's grateful you've come to do things for her,' he remarked smoothly.

Penelope shot a reproachful glance towards Maud. 'I wish I could agree with you. Really, I thought she'd have been *pleased* to see me——'

'But she wasn't?' he pursued.

'Not in the least. She was polite but firm. She thanked me for coming, but told me quite plainly that Maud was the only person who would be attending to her. *Maud*, and nobody else. Can you imagine anything more ridiculous?'

Maud spoke in an aggrieved tone. 'It is *not* ridiculous. I've always attended to her. She's used to me.'

Penelope ignored the remark as she continued to speak to Lance. 'Couldn't you talk to Nell and tell her to be sensible?'

'Nell's usually very sensible,' he replied mildly. 'What, exactly, did you say to her?'

Penelope took a deep breath, as though to emphasise her virtue.

'I tried to explain that I'd come here to help Maud, and she told me I could do that down in the kitchen. I felt I had to point out that I had not come here to peel potatoes, wash vegetables and—and work in the kitchen.'

The dark hazel eyes gleamed with amusement. 'I'm sure that she understood?'

'Understood? Would you believe she started to giggle? She giggled until her eyes and nose ran and she began to cough. I was afraid she'd become hysterical. She seemed to think it hilarious that Maud had ordered me to do such menial tasks.'

Janie was unable to resist a question. 'Who does them at home, Penelope? Your mother, perhaps?'

'Certainly not!' Penelope snapped at her. 'Naturally, we have a *servant*.' The words ended with a baleful glance towards Maud.

The corners of Lance's mouth twitched slightly, as he turned to Janie. 'Do you also object to peeling potatoes?'

She shook her head, smiling as she visualised the scene upstairs. 'I'd like a dollar for every potato I've peeled since leaving school. I'm happy enough to eat them, especially when Maud turns them into tasty potato balls to have with a lunch dish. How do you make them, Maud?' The question was really a means of steering the converation towards more congenial ground.

'Oh, they're quite easy,' Maud explained airily. 'You just mix two or three cups of mashed potatoes with a couple of heaped tablespoons of flour, a tablespoon of chopped parsley and a beaten egg. You make balls of the mixture, roll them in egg and breadcrumbs, then fry them slowly till they're golden brown.'

'You see how it is?' Lance said to Penelope, his tone gentle, as though explaining the obvious to a child. 'Maud puts the hand of an expert on everything she touches. She is Nell's very dear companion and she runs this house with smooth efficiency. She's also very *close* to Nell, so I doubt that she'll allow herself to be prized away from attending to her—if you can see the picture.'

Watching her, Janie realised that Penelope had no difficulty in seeing the picture. She noticed the dark eyes become thoughtful with the realisation that Maud's orders must be followed—or she could go home. And this, Janie guessed, was something Penelope had no intention of doing. At least, not yet.

Nor was it surprising when Penelope capitulated by turning to Maud with an apologetic smile. 'I'm sorry, Maud,' she said sweetly. '*Of course* I'll do the potatoes—I'll do *anything* you say.'

'Good girl,' Lance said softly, his eyes resting upon her face. 'Now that's what I call being really neighbourly.' He paused, then grinned as he added, 'However, there's no need to be in the kitchen by six in the morning to cook my breakfast, because I always get it myself.'

Penelope ignored his teasing as she gazed at him with an expression that was almost ardent. 'Oh, but I wouldn't mind at all—I'd *love* to cook your breakfast.'

I'll bet you would, Janie thought to herself, then knew a sense of relief when he persisted with his refusal.

When the meal was finished, Lance stretched his long length in an easy chair, while he read the newspaper which had been thrown from the paper delivery car as it had passed the drive entrance. Maud went upstairs to Nell, and Janie and Penelope cleared the table. Little was said as the plates were stacked into the dishwasher, and after switching on the machine Janie returned to her task of carding the wool.

Penelope did not offer to help. Instead, she wandered to

the sliding glass doors where she pushed back the long drapes and gazed at the moonlight casting shadows across the garden. 'It's a lovely night,' she said over her shoulder to Lance. 'There's no wind and the moon is full.' Then, pushing the door open she took a deep breath. 'There's perfume coming from everywhere. I'd love to walk in the garden to see the moonlight on the flowering cherries, but the dark shadows make me feel nervous—so—will you come with me?'

He rose obediently and without so much as a glance at Janie, followed Penelope outside.

Janie sighed and continued to card the locks of wool, placing each fluffy handful in a basket beside her. A tight knot of bitter jealousy began to form somewhere inside her, making her feel cold and miserable as she recalled that *she* had never been out in the moonlight with Lance. Would he take Penelope in his arms while they stood beneath the laden boughs of cherry blossoms? Would Penelope be held as closely as she herself had been held? Tears pricked at her lids, until she told herself to snap out of it.

But this became impossible as a sudden fear leapt into her mind—the fear that perhaps Lance would ask Penelope to marry him. The moonlit garden would be an idyllic setting for a declaration of love, and Janie felt a strong desire to leave the room before they returned. Imagination showed her the glow of triumph in Penelope's face, and she had no wish to see it in reality.

However, a hasty departure was prevented by the task before her. Maud needed the wool to be carded in readiness for spinning, and this was something she could do for her; therefore she continued to pick up each lock, attack it with the prickly hackle and place it neatly in the basket.

There was no sign of Lance and Penelope when the last fluffy handful had been placed in the basket, and, with nothing further to keep her in the living-room, she decided to go to bed. She climbed the stairs despondently, then went into Nell's room to say goodnight.

The small woman lay watching Maud, who sat nearby, her steel knitting needles flashing beneath the light, and as Janie entered they turned to look at her.

Maud's eyes held a question. 'You're going to bed so early?'

'Yes, I'm rather tired.' Then, hurriedly, 'I've finished carding that lot. You've plenty of wool to keep you spinning.'

Maud smiled gratefully. 'Thank you, dear. Did Penelope help you?'

'No, but it didn't matter.'

Nell's voice came huskily through her sore throat. 'What are Lance and Penelope doing?'

'They're walking in the garden. Penelope wanted to see the cherry trees by moonlight, especially as it's a full moon——' Janie's voice trailed away.

'How very romantic,' Maud sniffed. 'I can't help feeling afraid that she'll get him yet.'

'How many hours ago was that?' Nell quavered huskily.

'Oh, some time ago, I suppose,' Janie admitted reluctantly.

Maud and Nell looked at each other without speaking and, watching them, Janie saw their mouths tighten. Their silence, she realised, was more eloquent than anything they could have uttered. Therefore, to change the subject, she switched her attention to Nell. 'How are you feeling this evening?' she asked solicitously.

'Rotten,' Nell croaked. 'I'll be here tomorrow and the next day.'

'And the next and the next,' Maud added with decision.

A tear rolled down Nell's cheek. 'Maud, dear—what would I do without you?'

'Now, stop that nonsense,' Maud said briskly. 'You'll never have to even try.'

Janie left the two friends and went to her room, but before undressing she went out to stand on the balcony. The brilliant moonlight illuminated the garden, causing shrubs to stand as dark silhouettes, but of Lance and Penelope there was no sign, until the latter's voice floated up to her ears. The sound of it startled her and, leaning over the rail, she saw them standing directly below her.

'Do we have to go inside just yet?' Penelope asked plaintively. 'It's so lovely out here.'

'Haven't we left Janie alone for long enough?' Lance's deep tones came crisply.

'Good grief—don't tell me you're worrying about *her*!' The words were followed by a derisive laugh.

'To be honest, I feel somewhat remiss.'

'For heaven's sake—*why*?'

Standing above them, Janie was about to let her presence become known, but curiosity caused her to remain silent. Why did Lance feel remiss? And then the answer floated up to her.

'Because she could have come with us to see the cherry blossoms. Actually, I thought we'd only be outside for a few minutes.'

'I doubt that she'd have done so, even if you'd asked her.'

'Why not?' The question came sharply.

'Because she was engrossed in that all-important wool-carding. Keeping sweet with Maud—that's what she's doing. Besides, she knew perfectly well that you and I wanted to be alone.' She paused, obviously waiting for a response to this remark, but when none came she went on crossly, 'In any case, if she's so keen to see the moonlight on the cherry blossoms she can look through the bedroom window.'

'While you could have looked through *your* bedroom window.' Lance's voice sounded irritable.

But Penelope was persistent, her tones holding a pleading note. 'Lance, darling—can't you realise I wanted to have you to myself—and without *her*?'

He was still irritable. 'And can't you realise that I want you and Janie to be friends?'

'You're joking, of course.' The words were snapped angrily.

'I've never been more serious, Pen,' he drawled.

'Then you had better understand that I'm not even remotely interested in Janine Meredith. I see no point in becoming the close friend of someone who'll be here for such a short time.'

'What makes you so sure it'll be for only a short time?'

'Because Peter Bryant will be back sooner than you think.'

'How do you know?' His tone held surprise.

'Mother has spoken to him. She phoned his home to inquire about his progress. Just a neighbourly gesture, of course——'

'Of course.' The words, uttered drily, were accompanied by a short laugh. 'I must say I've never known her to be solicitous about neighbouring staff. So, what did she learn?'

'He told her his injuries were healing well, and that he's just itching to get back to work. When he's back on the job, Janine will leave—so why should I bother about being friendly?'

'I thought it would have been automatic. It's not difficult to be friendly with Janie, because she's such a sweet girl.'

'Is she, indeed?' Penelope retorted angrily. 'Personally I consider her to be a scheming little madam. Just look at the cunning way in which she got herself into this house.'

'Yet I couldn't have done without her.' His words seemed to be accompanied by a sigh.

'That's utter rubbish,' Penelope exclaimed, her voice rising with exasperation. 'You had Sid Brown and Don Watson—and—and *you had me*——'

'The three of you all having one thing in common,' he interrupted.

'Oh? What do you mean?'

'Do I have to remind you again? You're all as rough as the devil on a horse's mouth—and that's something I'll not tolerate.'

Penelope's voice, full of indignation, faded as they moved to enter the living-room door.

Janie remained standing still on the moon-drenched balcony. She knew she'd been eavesdropping shamelessly, but felt no remorse as she thought over what had been said. The most interesting part, she decided, concerned Peter Bryant, who was apparently on the mend and anxious to get back to work—and this meant that the end of her job was in sight, because the moment he returned she'd have no further reason for remaining at Golden Hills.

Depressed by the thought, she undressed slowly, then lay wide-eyed in a darkness broken by shafts of moonlight coming through the glass doors. Further snippets of the overheard conversation flashed into her mind, and she found herself puzzled by Lance's desire for friendship to become established between Penelope and herself. However, she brushed it aside as she recalled he'd referred to her as a sweet girl. It was little enough praise, but it lifted her spirits and gave her comfort. Her eyes closed and she slept.

CHAPTER NINE

NELL's 'flu hung upon her for a week, but at last, with Maud's loving care and attention, it began to abate. By the middle of the following week she was sitting up in bed, knitting, and declaring she was ready to come downstairs.

Penelope continued to remain at Golden Hills, and made no move to go home when Nell finally joined them in the living-room. By that time, both Nell and Maud had come to know her a little better, and seemed resigned to accepting her presence.

'At least she's been helpful in the house,' Maud admitted with reluctance.

Janie nodded, but said nothing. She had seen Penelope being helpful when Nell had sent her to the lounge for a pattern book that had been left on the mantelpiece above the wide open fireplace. Penelope had been dusting ornaments in the large room, peering at the base of each one in an effort to ascertain its value.

'I love good ornaments,' she'd said, on realising her interest in them was being observed. 'This one is Spode.'

'Then don't drop it,' Janie had warned.

'I'm not likely to do that,' Penelope had retorted coldly. 'I'll *always* look after each one of them when——' She fell silent.

'Always? When? What are you talking about?' Janie had been unable to resist the questions.

'You know what I'm talking about,' Penelope had replied with a lofty smile.

The insinuation that she was referring to the time when she and Lance were married had the effect of making Janie

149

feel cold, but apart from that small incident she knew little of what Penelope did in the house, because she herself was kept busy with the polo ponies.

During the week, she was without Lance's help, because at long last the shearers had arrived. The gang had installed itself in the shearers' quarters, which were equipped to accommodate them, and the area round the woolshed echoed to the bleating of the flock. Lambs, separated from their mothers while the latter were being shorn, kept up a din that was equal to hundreds of loudly yelling babies.

Janie approached the shed, riding Joy and leading Gay. She could see Sid Brown moving sheep from one railed yard to another, while Don drove a small mob of ewes up a ramp towards the shed's interior pens. To ride on without looking inside was impossible, therefore she tethered the ponies and went up the front steps of the woolshed.

Standing just inside the wide open doorway, she drank in the familiar scene of shearing, her eyes resting on the line of four shearers in their sleeveless black vests. She watched as sheep were dragged in backwards through low swinging doors, and saw the shearers bend over them while electrically driven handpieces moved over the woolly animals.

The men worked rapidly. Short, careful strokes and long expert sweeps removed the fleeces which were then gathered up and thrown over a table, where they landed in one unbroken mat to have soiled wool skirted from their edges. They were then rolled and placed in bins located along one wall.

Lance was busy carrying rolls from the bins to the woolpress, which was lined with a woolpack in readiness to receive them. He watched a completed bale being removed from the press, then came towards her. By that time, nostalgic memories were boring into her brain, causing tears to gather in her eyes. She brushed them away rapidly as he drew near.

He observed the damp patches on her cheeks, then accused, 'You've been weeping, Blue-eyes. Has Penelope been getting at you?'

She was surprised. 'Are you saying you actually realise she gets at me? I haven't complained about it.'

'You don't have to. Do you think I'm blind and deaf? What was the trouble this time?'

She shook her head. 'Nothing to do with Penelope. I'm just being stupid. You could call it a longing for my old home.'

He nodded, his eyes full of sympathy. 'I can understand how you feel. Would you believe I used to suffer from the same malady when I was in the South Island?'

'But you knew you could come home—whereas I'm unable to do so.'

'Then you'll have to do something about it,' he remarked lazily, at the same time drawing her out to the landing, where the noise of the shearing machines was not quite so loud.

She looked at him wonderingly. 'Do something? I don't understand. What could I possibly do about returning to my old home?'

'The place is leased, isn't it? Leases don't go on for ever.'

'So—what are you saying?'

'No doubt the time will come when you'll marry a farmer—someone who could take over the lease—if you get my drift.'

She turned to face him squarely, the mocking glint in his eyes causing a flush of anger to rise to her cheeks. 'Are you suggesting I should marry a farmer for what he could give me?'

'At least he'd put you back in your old environment. You haven't been able to fool me, Janie. You've been bitten by the nostalgia bug ever since you've been here.'

'I've loved being here——'

'Only because it's been so like your previous existence—farm life with polo ponies to ride. Now, be honest.'

'That is not entirely correct. I've also loved being here because of Nell and Maud—but your suggestion that I'd consider marrying a man for the sake of living on a farm—my old home, or any other place—*is an insult*. I had no idea you thought so little of me—although I should have known you'd expect me to *cheat*,' she concluded bitterly, her eyes clouding as the knowledge caused a sense of shock.

'I didn't say that.' He was watching her intently.

'But you meant it.' The accusation came hotly. 'So, let me tell you this, Lance Winter—I would never marry a man unless I loved him. *Never*—do you understand? In fact I doubt that I'll *ever* marry!' She almost choked over the last words, as tears welled into her eyes once more.

His dark brows drew together as he stared at her. 'You're in love with someone who's already married?'

'Of course not!' she snapped in a fury.

'Then why, at your age, would you make such a statement?'

'Because—because——' She looked away from him, blinking rapidly and being unable to find further words.

'Perhaps the man you love—loves somebody else?' he prompted, his voice unexpectedly gentle.

'Yes, that's it.' She snatched at a reason that sounded as though it could be feasible, then turned away from him.

'I think you're a liar,' he said softly. 'Who is this fellow?'

'That's not your business.' She was still unable to look at him.

'I'm *making* it my business.' A hard note had crept into his voice as he gripped her arm and twisted her round to face him.

'You can ask till your face turns purple!' she snapped

heatedly. 'I shan't tell you nor can I see why it should interest you. As far as I can see, you're on the verge of becoming engaged to Penelope.' Seething jealousy began to churn within her.

He appeared to be startled. 'On the verge, eh? What makes you imagine it's so close?'

'The fact that she's still at Golden Hills, of course. She knows Nell is well again, but does she make a move to go home? Oh no—she doesn't. And why not? Because she knows you want her to be there.' She stopped, appalled by her own outburst. 'I'm sorry, I know it's not my business.'

He regarded her closely. 'You appear to resent her presence. I'd be interested to know why.'

'If you don't mind—I'd rather not talk about her.'

'I do mind—so please tell me.' He persisted.

She sighed. 'Very well, if you *must* know—I'll admit I'm tired of being treated like a second-rate member of the household. Her superior attitude towards me and her snide remarks are inclined to get under my skin. But I suppose I can put up with it until Peter Bryant returns, because then I'll be leaving.'

He ignored her last words by saying, 'Nell and Maud appear to be getting along quite nicely with her.'

Janie smiled, but said nothing.

'Well, aren't they? Please tell me,' he demanded with a touch of irritation.

'Very well indeed—when you're around.'

'What's that supposed to mean?'

'Really, Lance—I've no wish to talk about her, but if you will insist upon dragging it out of me, you might as well know there's been tension through young Sam going into the kitchen and emptying the cookie tins. Maud wouldn't mind if he took just one or two—but he fills his pockets and takes the lot. But perhaps I shouldn't be telling these tales on your—your future stepson.'

'I prefer to know what's going on in my own house. Hasn't Maud complained about Sam's antics? His mother should be told.'

Janie gave a mirthless laugh. 'Oh, yes—Maud complained in loud, clear tones. But Penelope merely declared that while she was at Golden Hills the boy had every right to be there, too—and as he was in the habit of emptying the cookie tins at home, he no doubt thought he could do so here. After all, he was regarding the place as his *second home.*'

She paused, waiting for him to comment on her last words, but he said nothing; therefore her voice became gentle as she said, 'I know you meant well, Lance, but I'm afraid it hasn't worked.'

His eyes held a puzzled expression. 'What hasn't worked?'

'Your plans for better relations between neighbours. The personality clashes are still there, even if kept hidden below the surface. It makes the situation difficult for you—especially when you're in love with Penelope.'

She waited anxiously for him to deny her last words, but again he made no reply. Instead, his eyes gazed thoughtfully towards the hills, his silence seeming to confirm the fact of his love for Penelope.

An intense sadness began to grow within her, but before it could manifest itself on her face she swung round and ran down the steps to where the two fillies had been left. Tears were beginning to blur her vision as she swung a leg over Gay's saddle, and it was necessary to blink them away before she could see where she was going.

Shearing lasted for a week and, during the period, Janie found difficulty in keeping away from the woolshed. Nevertheless, she was meticulous about her time spent with the ponies, and if Lance noticed her visits between the exercising sessions he made no comment. He did not stop to talk to her, nor did she expect him to do so.

Watching his activities as he moved between the shearers, she crossed the floor to raise her voice above the din of the machines. 'Is there anything I can do to help?'

'Yes, I'd be glad if you'd tell Don that number four pen inside the shed is nearly empty. Perhaps you could help him to shove them along——'

A quick survey showed her that pens number two and three were also only half-full. Making her way down the loading ramp, she began to assist Don in getting more sheep into the shed. She knew the inner pens had to be kept full, otherwise the shearers were given extra work in catching and dragging the animals out to the machines, and she was delighted to be part of the job.

She didn't see much of Lance during the evenings of that week. He came in hot and dusty, then showered and changed before relaxing with a glass of Scotch in his hand, but when the meal was over he disappeared into his office.

At last, the shearing was finished. The large, square bales were loaded on to trucks which took them to Napier where they would await the next wool sales. The shearing gang departed, and life seemed to be back to normal.

At the end of the last day, Nell smiled across the table at Lance. 'Well, that's it for another year. Thank you for all those lovely fleeces, dear. I intend to give a couple to Janie's mother in appreciation for the help she's given us.'

'That's OK—they'll keep you all busy,' he said absently, his mind appearing to be elsewhere. Then, after a few thoughtful moments he turned to Penelope. 'I didn't see you at the woolshed.'

She was startled. 'Did you expect to see me there?'

'Janie was there every day. She even helped Don.'

Penelope sent him a superior smile. 'Oh well, I suppose it's all right for Janine. She's probably used to dust and flies and noise and—and *smells*. I'm afraid I'm much too fastidious for that sort of activity. I'm really *above* it.'

'I see. Don't you ever go into your father's woolshed?'

'Certainly not!' The words came sharply, then she smiled as she said, 'I prefer the beautiful clear air like—like the evening air in the garden. Shall we walk out to see the cherry blossoms again? The flowers are beginning to fade and drop.' She looked at him hopefully.

'Not this evening,' he said quietly.

'Please, Lance—their life is so short,' she pleaded.

He shook his head. 'I'll be busy in my office.'

'You've been there every evening this week,' Penelope complained.

'That's right. I've been attending to accounts, and I've also been working on a small project for Janie. I'll finish it this evening.'

His words came as a surprise to everyone, especially to Janie. 'For me?' she almost squeaked.

Penelope looked annoyed. 'What sort of project could you be working on for Janine?' she demanded.

He laughed as he left the table. 'You'll just have to wait and see,' was all he said.

Nell sent a thoughtful look towards Janie. 'I wonder—is it possible?'

Maud appeared to read her thoughts. 'Of course it's possible.'

Penelope became exasperated. 'What on earth are you talking about?' she demanded, looking from one to the other.

Nell said, 'I could be wrong, so we'd better wait and see. I'd hate to raise Janie's hopes and then see her disappointed.'

They didn't have long to wait, because Lance returned within a short time. He carried several hand-written pages, which he placed on Janie's lap. 'There you are,' he grinned. 'Look upon it as a bonus for work in the shed.'

She stared down at the papers, then raised questioning

eyes to his. 'What is it?' she queried, almost afraid to ask, and struggling to keep the excitement from her voice.

'You'll see when you read the heading. If you don't read it aloud, everyone will burst with curiosity.'

She looked at the top of page one, her eyes almost blurring and her voice shaking slightly as she read the words, '"Polo Abroad. Reminiscences told to Janine Meredith."'

Penelope was dismayed. 'Good grief, Lance! You're actually giving her an interview! Well, really, after all you've had to say about it——' she exclaimed crossly.

Lance sent her a cool glance. 'Janie *hasn't* interviewed me. It's really an article I've written about a few incidents overseas, but it can be presented as an article. Actually, I've enjoyed doing it.'

Penelope became scornful. 'What makes you think it'll go in exactly as you've written it? I'll bet she alters and chops it about——'

Janie was scanning the pages. 'I don't think there's any need for editing,' she said. 'It's well written. I'm sure the editor will be pleased with it.' She was savouring the joys of sweet triumph. Her eyes shone and she was conscious of an inner excitement, Lance had actually written the article she wanted, yet she hesitated to display her intense satisfaction, in case it made her appear to be gloating over Penelope.

When she had finished the last page, she raised her eyes to meet his and, knowing he awaited her comment, she said, 'It flows easily and holds the interest. Have you any photos that can be sent with it?'

He nodded. 'I've already looked out a few.'

Penelope gave a short laugh. 'I hope you don't expect to have them returned to you.'

'I have the negatives,' he informed her nonchalantly. 'Tell me—why are you being so bitchy, Penelope?'

Her answer came with suppressed anger. 'Because I consider you've been tricked into writing this story.'

'Tricked? By whom?' His brow darkened.

'By Janine, of course. She's persuaded you in some cunning way of her own until she's broken down your defences. You know you've always refused to give interviews—you've been adamant about it—yet there you are, handing it to her on a plate.'

Lance's voice became icy. 'Aren't you forgetting that this is something written by me? I thought about it until I decided to see how it looked on paper—and once I got started I began to enjoy digging up various incidents that had happened on the field.'

Penelope laughed. 'Wait till you see it in print,' she jeered. 'It will have been completely changed.'

Janie became indignant as she rose to the magazine's defence. 'You're being unjust, Penelope. The editor has never altered or even cut any of my work, and there's no reason for him to do so with this.'

'Huh. That's what *you* say——' Penelope sneered.

Nell sat up straight and glared at Penelope. Her voice became sharp as she said, 'Well, really—I shall not tolerate such rudeness to my guest. You can either apologise, or go to bed.'

Penelope was startled by Nell's unexpected attack. She flushed slightly, mumbled something inaudible and lapsed into silence.

Janie decided to ignore her. She turned to Lance and said, 'Would you like to see it typed? I could do it now.'

Lance turned to Janie. 'You actually have a typewriter here?'

She nodded. 'It's a portable, and it's been in the boot of my car ever since my arrival. I hadn't bothered to take it upstairs,' she added, hoping that this would help to convince him of the fact that she had decided against trying to interview him.

He appeared to give thought to her words, then he said, 'Fetch your car keys. You can use the typewriter on the desk in my office.'

Maud, who had been silent for a long time, now spoke to Lance, smiling at him as she said, 'When it's typed, you'll be able to check that it is being sent *exactly* as you've written it, and without alterations made to it—as Penelope suggests.' She appeared to be pleased with the turn of events.

Nell also wore an air of satisfaction. She looked at Lance pleadingly. 'When it's typed, would you read it aloud to us? Maud and I would love to know what you've said—and I'm sure Penelope would also be interested.'

But Penelope merely shrugged and said nothing.

Janie stood up quickly. She left her room, and as she ran up the stairs to fetch her car keys she felt almost light-headed. The fact that she was about to type the article she had wanted was almost unbelievable, but became more real a short time later when she sat at Lance's desk.

It was the first time she'd been in his office, which was a small room beyond the lounge and on the end of the house. A quick glance showed her that, apart from the large roll-top desk and a couple of chairs, it held little more than a filing cabinet and bookshelves. A door leading out to a side veranda enabled Lance to enter or leave his office without going through the house.

She watched as he placed the typewriter on the desk and adjusted the long arm of the desk-lamp. The actions made her turn to him impulsively, and looking up at him she said, 'Thank you for doing this story, Lance—I'm so grateful for it.'

'Then suppose you thank me in the proper manner, Blue-eyes.'

She raised her face obediently to place a kiss on his cheek.

'Is that the best you can do?' he demanded, his voice low, his eyes shadowed.

She raised her face again, this time brushing his lips with her own, then a gasp escaped her as he snatched her to him.

'Are you without arms?' he whispered huskily in her ear.

Her arms went up to entwine about his neck, and she found herself clinging to him while a miscellany of desperate thoughts shot through her mind, darting madly in a variety of directions. Was this to be the last time she'd feel the strength of his hands pressing her against the length of his body? Were these kisses to be the final ones to trail across her brow and cheeks before his lips found hers?

And then Peter Bryant's name rose to mock her, warning that the day of his return must be drawing near. When that day came, it would be goodbye Golden Hills, and as the knowledge pierced her brain she clung to him with even more desperation.

Her uninhibited response to his nearness caused his kiss to deepen, and as her lips parted, his mounting desire to possess her body made him gasp, causing her to tremble in his arms.

Against her mouth he murmured, 'Janie—my darling——' But almost before the words had been uttered his hands moved to grip her shoulders and push her away. His movements were unexpectedly firm, and even as she gaped at him he muttered, 'You'd better get on with the job.' He then stepped away, to stare at the darkness beyond the window.

His abrupt actions were like a sudden rejection of her, the shock of it causing her to sink into the chair before the desk. Her mind groped blindly for a reason—and then Penelope's voice hit her ears. She then realised that Lance had heard the sound of an approach, whereas she herself had not.

The tall, dark-haired woman stood in the doorway, the

desk-lamp causing her eyes to glitter as she surveyed them. Her voice, when at last she spoke, held a note of possessiveness.

'Lance, dear—Janine will find difficulty in concentrating if you persist in remaining in the room. You'll cause her to make typing errors.'

He turned slowly to face her. 'You have something in mind?'

'Of course—the cherry blossoms. I'm still anxious to take a last look at them before they fall, so please come out into the garden with me. I'm a little nervous of the dark,' she ended, crossing the room to clasp his hand and drew him towards the doorway.

He appeared to hesitate for the barest second, before taking a deep breath and conceding to her wishes. 'Very well—I suppose they'll finish any day now.' He glanced at Janie. 'You're OK? You have everything you need?'

She nodded, unable to speak as she watched him leave the room with Penelope, and the moment she was alone she was overcome by a deep despondency, which rapidly changed to a mounting anger. The *temerity* of him to kiss her in a manner that drew such a revealing response from herself, and then—*almost immediately*—to take Penelope out to the moonlit cherry trees! Of course, it was his way of warning her that the kisses meant *nothing* to him—*absolutely nothing*. How *dared* he kiss her like that and not mean it?

Yet she had almost imagined she'd detected sincerity in his embrace, and it was this that had caused her to be idiotic enough to bask in the joy of being held close to him. Why did she become weak-kneed and like a jelly every time he touched her? The answer to that was simple. She just couldn't help herself.

Tears blurred her vision a she rolled papers and carbon into the typewriter. She dabbed at her eyes impatiently, her wispy handkerchief becoming a damp ball in her hand, then tried to concentrate, while her fingers hit the keys with more force than necessary. But her mind remained in an agitated whirl, causing her to make typing errors until she was forced to snatch the papers from the machine and begin again.

It was almost an hour before she was finished, and by that time she had read it several times, searching for errors caused by her lack of concentration. Eventually she returned to the living-room, where she found Nell and Maud busy at their spinning-wheels, while Lance and Penelope watched television from the settee.

Janie was struck by the satisfied expression on the latter's face, and as she wondered about it a vague feeling of uneasiness grew within her. Could it mean that Lance had kissed her beneath the cherry trees? She tried to brush the thought aside as she handed the papers to him.

He had risen to his feet when she'd come into the room, and as he took the papers from her his eyes scanned her face. 'You look unhappy. Is there something wrong with it?'

She took herself in hand, forcing a smile. 'Oh, no, I think it's more than satisfactory. Now then—this is your hand-written script from which you can check that I've typed exactly what you've written.'

'I see. Thank you.' He took it from her.

'This is the top copy to be sent to the editor—and this is the carbon copy for you to keep. It will enable you to check whether or not the published story is as you wrote it.'

'You're being very meticulous.'

'In this case, I'm finding it to be most necessary.' She continued to regard him steadily. 'I have also addressed an envelope for you. When you've read the typed version, you can seal it and keep it with you until it is posted. In that way, I'll be unable to tamper with it or make alterations—

as has been suggested.' She flashed a glance towards Penelope.

The latter was still looking pleased with herself. 'I really didn't mean it,' she said sweetly and with a disarming smile.

'No? You could have fooled me,' Janie replied quietly.

Nell said, 'We're waiting to hear what you've written, Lance. Aren't you going to read it to us?'

The television was then switched off, and the spinning-wheels became still, as he settled himself on the arm of the settee and began to read about amusing incidents and experiences that had occurred on overseas polo fields. They listened attentively, and when it was finished Nell and Maud expressed approval, while Penelope became more than enthusiastic.

'Lance, dear,' she gushed, 'That's *most* interesting! I had no idea you could put words together so well. I'm *so* glad you've written it—it's *much* better than if Janine had tried to write it.' She pulled herself up and turned to Janie with an impulsive show of friendship. 'Lance is being so *marvellous* to me——'

'Oh? In what way?' Janie's brows rose as a mixture of questions raced through her mind. Here it comes, she thought— '*we're about to become engaged*' —as though it hadn't been obvious all along! And then Penelope's next words came as a surprise.

'He's allowing me to have Sam to stay for a few nights. He'll sleep in the other single bed in my room. Don't you think that's *kind* of him? Of course Sam *adores* this place, and Lance *knows* Sam looks upon him as a father figure,' she added, with a roguish laugh that was meant to suggest the words had been spoken in jest.

Janie could think of nothing to say. She sent a veiled peep towards Lance, but his expressionless face told her nothing.

But Maud's interest had been caught and her wheel came to a stop as she asked a question. 'Where is the boy's own father, Penelope? Has he no access to him?'

Penelope hesitated for several moments before she answered, but at last she said, 'Oh yes, he comes to see him occasionally.' She paused again, then admitted, 'Actually he's keen for us to get together again.' The last words were accompanied by a sly glance towards Lance.

Watching her, Janie smiled inwardly. She's trying to make him jealous, she thought. But if Penelope's words registered with Lance he gave no sign.

Nell's wheel had now also become still. 'That would be very good for Sam,' she said. 'Every boy needs his own father, therefore I hope you're considering it seriously.'

'Indeed I am *not!*' Penelope declared with decison. 'As it happens, I have other plans.' She smiled, as though nursing a pleasant secret, but if she hoped to invite further questions concerning her future plans she was to be disappointed, because neither Nell nor Maud showed the slightest interest. Instead, their wheels began to whirl again.

Penelope then turned to Lance, her face eager, her dark eyes glowing. 'Lance, dear—didn't you hear what Nell said?'

He paused in perusing the typed pages. 'No, I'm afraid I wasn't listening. What did she say?'

'She said that Sam needs a *father.*' Penelope looked at him expectantly, a smile playing about her lips.

'She's right, of course. Every lad needs a dad. I personally know what it is like to be a boy without a father, although Nell's husband did his best for me.' His eyes seemed to look into the past as he added, 'I'll always be grateful to him.'

'And Sam will always be grateful to *you.*' Penelope declared earnestly, as she gazed into his face.

He turned to regard her with a hint of surprise. 'Oh? Why should he be grateful to me?'

'Because you're always so *kind* to him.' She took a deep breath then pleaded, 'When he's here during the next few days, will you promise to be a real father to him?'

He grinned. 'You mean, tan his young backside every time he happens to cross my path?'

She became indignant. 'Certainly not. Why should you do that?'

'Because, if a boy isn't just coming out of mischief, he'll be just going into it.'

'You're joking, of course,' she pouted.

Janie had listened to their conversaation with interest, her eyes becoming thoughtful as they rested upon Penelope. Were subtle means being used to force a commitment from Lance? Would he promise to be a father to Sam? And if he made such a promise before witnesses such as Nell, Maud and herself, would he feel obliged to carry it through to the point of actually becoming the boy's stepfather?

To her relief, no such promise was made, because Lance's interest returned to the pages he still held in his hand, and after another short persual they were folded and sealed into the addressed envelope. He then switched on the television and relaxed to watch whatever appeared on the screen.

Penelope didn't say anything further on the subject and, watching her, Janie realised she had achieved her objective. She had let Lance know that she wished him to be a father to her son, and she had also imparted the news of her ex-husband's desire to renew their former relationship. Obviously it was all she could do under the present circumstances, but no doubt the topic would be raised again when they were alone.

It was late during the next afternoon when Sam arrived. Janie had finished her day's work with the polo ponies, and was in her bedroom when he carried his small suitcase upstairs to the room occupied by his mother.

He spoke to her from the doorway. 'Did you see my new pony?'

She turned to smile at him. 'Yes, I noticed him in the stable paddock. What's his name?'

'Rainbow. It's a sissy name, but Grandpa says I'm not to change it. I'll just call him Rain.'

'Is he nice to ride?'

'He can go faster than Tinker.'

'So what happens to Tinker?'

'Uncle Lance has got it all fixed. He paid Grandpa money for him.'

Janie was puzzled. 'Lance bought Tinker? Why would he do that?'

'He said Sid Brown has children smaller than me. Tinker will have a good home, and I can see him any time I like. Those kids better ride him proper,' he added fiercely.

'I'm sure they will,' she said, appreciating Lance's generosity towards his manager's children.

Sam went on, 'Grandma says it's a good idea, 'cause when Mum and Uncle Lance get married there'll be more small children.'

His words sent a quiver of shock through Janie. Was this the real reason for Lance's purchase of Tinker?

Sam came further into the room. He stood looking about him, then went through the balcony door to gaze at the ocean. 'You can see the beach from here,' he remarked wistfully. 'You can't see it from Mum's room. I wish I could sleep in this room.' He paused to look at her hopefully. 'How about we swap beds?'

Janie laughed. 'No, thank you very much.'

'I like this room,' he said. 'When Mum marries Uncle Lance I'll sleep in here.' His dark eyes stared at her through wisps of black fringe. 'How long you gonna be here?' he demanded belligerently.

'For as long as Uncle Lance needs me,' she told him lightly. 'Probably until Peter Bryant is back at work.' She looked at the boy thougthfully, and then intuition put an idea into her head. It was strong enough to make her say, 'You were there when he fell, weren't you, Sam?'

A long silence followed the question, until at last he said, 'How do you know?'

'Oh, it's easy to guess about it. But—*you were there*?'

'Yeah, I was there.' He looked away from her.

'How did it happen?'

Sam's cheeks became pink as he shuffled his feet and said nothing.

'You *know* what made him fall, don't you, Sam?' Janie persisted.

The boy hung his head and continued to remain silent.

Janie sighed. 'Oh, well, I suppose we'll learn all about it quite soon. When Peter Bryant comes back he'll tell us exactly what happened.'

Sam's head jerked up as he glared at her defiantly. 'He tried to drag me out of the loft.'

'But you refused to go?'

'You bet I refused to go! Uncle Lance is the boss—not him. Then he grabbed my arm and dragged me towards the stairs.' He paused, his eyes wide, as though reviewing the scene.'

'Go on,' Janie prompted. 'What happened then?'

'When he got me to the top of the stairs I fought like crazy. I twisted and struggled, then I bit his hand *hard*. I kicked him on the front of his legs and he called me names. That's when he stepped back and fell down the stairs.'

'He could have broken his back—or his neck,' Janie pointed out.

Sam gave a slight shrug. 'Serve him right,' he muttered sulkily. 'When I'm boss of this place I'll give him the sack. I'll tell him to *get down the road*—just like Grandpa tells people.'

Janie said, 'Does your mother know about this?'

Sam nodded. 'She found me crying in bed because I was

frightened about what Uncle Lance would say. She promised not to tell him.' He looked at her apprehensively. 'Are you gonna tell him?'

Janie shook her head. 'No, I think I can quite safely leave that job in Peter Bryant's hands.' And then she recalled something Penelope had said the previous evening. Looking at the boy, curiosity made her ask, 'Have you seen your father recently, Sam?'

He nodded. 'He came to see me just before Mum came to live here.'

She was startled. 'Mum has come—to *live* here?'

'Grandma says she's come to live here—so I suppose she has.'

'Oh.' Then, reverting to her former question, 'Do you like your father, Sam?'

Sam shrugged. 'He's OK, I suppose. He brings me presents—and he's got a big car. Grandpa says it cost the earth. I saw him try to kiss Mum,' he added unexpectedly.

'You did?' Janie was intrigued by the information. 'I wonder if she kissed him in return.'

Sam shook his head. 'No. She told him she was going to marry Uncle Lance.'

CHAPTER TEN

JANIE told herself she was being an utter fool to allow an eight-year old boy's words to upset her. Penelope had not moved in permanently, and it was merely wishful thinking on Sam's part. Nevertheless, as the days passed, his mother showed no sign of leaving.

Her continued presence did not please Nell and, while the small woman presented a calm exterior, her agitation simmered below the surface. 'How long does Penelope intend to stay here?' she fretted to Maud when Janie happened to be with them.

Maud sighed as she made an effort to console her. 'Don't let it worry you. Sooner or later matters will sort themselves out.'

'Oh, yes? Just tell me when?' Nell demanded.

'Things will come to a head—just you wait and see.'

'I notice she no longer does half the things you ask her to do,' Nell pointed out in an aggrieved tone. 'She's beginning to ignore your requests in that supercilious manner of hers. In fact, she's becoming quite *bossy*. Really, I can't understand Lance. Why doesn't he tell her to *go home?*'

Maud smiled. 'You, of all people should know the answer to that question,' she told Nell.

'I suppose you're right.' The admission came with reluctance. 'It would be like saying thank you for your help, but now we no longer need you, so please go home.'

'Exactly,' Maud agreed. 'Lance is the last person to take that attitude towards a person who's been helpful, so I'm afraid we'll just have to wait and see what happens.'

'Isn't it possible he doesn't want her to go home?' Janie asked.

'To be honest, I don't know what to think,' Maud admitted.

But it seemed as if nothing would happen. As each day passed, Penelope and her son appeared to become more firmly entrenched at Golden Hills.

This situation is ridiculous, Janie thought crossly, although she could understand that what Nell and Maud had said was indeed a fact. For Lance to tell Penelope to go home would be a shabby way of repaying her for the help she'd given them, nor was it the way in which he would act. She's got him under an obligation and she's making full use of it, Janie decided, fuming inwardly.

However, the end of shearing had brought the daily routine with the four polo ponies back to normal. Lance was again riding over the hills with her, and she was conscious of a quiet joy as she followed his instruction in the exercise programme. And, while he made no attempt to kiss her in the haybarn or in the stable, there was a deepening companionship between them.

October slid into November and the days became warmer. The garden's spring flowers gave way to pink, red and purple rhododendrons, while the roses burst into bloom. The sun took the chill from the sea breezes and the cape pigeons wheeled against the blue sky.

If the days were pleasant the evenings were marred for Janie by Penelope's continued presence, as mother and son vied with each other for Lance's attention. However, it was usually Sam who managed to sit beside him on the settee, and when Lance helped the boy with arithmetic Penelope almost purred with satisfaction.

'Just look at them with their heads together,' she remarked happily to Nell. 'The colour of their hair is so similar they could be father and son.'

Sam's ears had caught her words. He looked up at Lance and said, 'Grandma told me about fathers and sons. She said that when Mum——'

'Be quiet, Sam,' Penelope snapped sharply. 'Never mind about what Grandma says. Just pay attention to that sum Uncle Lance is doing with you. Is it division or subtraction?' She added on a lighter note.

Lance looked at her reprovingly. 'Give the boy a chance to speak. Actually, I'm quite interested.'

'You are?' Her eyes held a sudden glow.

He turned to Sam. 'What does Grandma say, old chap?'

Sam grinned at him, delighted to find Uncle Lance on his side. 'Grandma says that when you and Mum are married I'll have a stepfather. Grandpa says, "And a jolly good job, too."'

Penelope's face turned crimson. 'You little wretch—Grandma said nothing of the sort!' she hissed.

'*She did so!*' Sam flared angrily. And she said it's *about time*!' The last words were shouted at his mother.

Penelope made an effort to control herself. She took a deep breath as she glanced nervously from Nell to Maud, and at last she said, 'I hope nobody in this room is silly enough to believe a word of what this child says. His imagination works overtime, and he's inclined to tell lies——'

'I am not telling lies,' Sam protested furiously. 'Grandma says——'

'*Shut up, Sam!*' his mother hooted.

Lance looked across the room with an amused glint in his eyes. 'Just a moment, Penelope. I'd like to hear the full story.' He turned to the boy. 'Now then, Sam—what does Grandma say?'

Sam took a quick glance at his mother's warning glare, but the importance of being centre stage was too much to be denied. He then proceeded to prove the old adage of little pitchers having big ears by recounting what he'd heard being said at home.

Thinking carefully, he said, 'Grandma says, when Mum marries Uncle Lance the wedding will be in the garden.

The gardener man has been getting it all fixed—he's been there extra days——'

'Dear heaven.' Penelope sighed in desperation.

'And Grandma says that Mum will wear a big hat. She's gotta come out from under that place where all the purple stuff hangs.'

'You mean the wistaria archway?' Nell asked.

'Yeah. I'm not allowed to climb up it till after the wedding.'

Maud glanced at Penelope. 'We knew the gardener was giving your parents' place extra days, but we hadn't guessed the reason.' Her voice was a little shaky.

Nell said in all seriousness, 'But surely the wistaria blossoms must have fallen by now, haven't they, Sam?'

'Yeah—that purple stuff is making a mess all over the path, but Grandma says not to worry. She's got it all fixed.'

'She has?' Lance's eyes twinkled.

'Yeah. She says she'll move everything over to the roses.'

'Good for her!' Lance chuckled. 'Now there's a woman who refuses to be beaten. The only trouble will be the circumstances beyond her control.'

'What are the circ—circ—what you said?' Sam demanded.

'They're devils that jump out and snap at your plans. I can see it's time your mother and I had a serious talk.'

Penelope's dark eyes shone. 'Do you really mean that, Lance?'

'Of course I mean it.'

'Then—I'm ready to listen,' she said softly. 'Mother will be quite delighted.' The words were accompanied by a small smile of triumph, directed towards Nell and Maud.

So there it was, Janie thought bitterly, her spirits plummeting to zero as she realised it had been brought about so easily by Sam's revelations. Of course Grandma would be delighted, and the only point Janie was unable to understand was Lance's reference to circumstances beyond her control. But at that precise moment she felt so dejected she was unable to think clearly about anything. And then her thoughts were diverted by the sound of a knock on the door leading out to the veranda.

Nell turned to Lance. 'Are you expecting a visitor?'

'Yes, Peter Bryant's out of hospital. He said he'd drop in for a short time. He's bringing accident insurance papers for me to sign.'

Penelope stood up hastily. 'I'll put Sam to bed——'

'No, you won't—you'll make him stay and face Peter.' Lance's tone snapped crisply as he crossed the room to open the door.

The man who stood on the veranda was slightly built and of medium height. One sleeve of his jacket hung loosely, and beneath it could be seen a plaster-encased arm. As he came through the door, Sam gave a muffled gasp then fled from the room. They heard him pounding up the stairs.

Penelope sent an apologetic glance towards Lance. 'I'd better go to him,' was all she said as she followed her son.

Janie was then introduced to Peter Bryant, who appeared to be about Lance's age. His grey eyes held undisguised admiration as he said, 'I'm told you've been holding the fort for me.'

She smiled. 'Yes, but please don't think I've taken your job. It's only until you're fit enough to return to work, and then I'll go home.' Perhaps never to come back, she thought sadly.

Possibly it was the expression on her face that made him turn to Lance. 'You'll let her slip through your fingers, boss?'

Lance evaded the question. 'By the look of that plaster, she'll be here longer than expected.'

Peter's eyes twinkled as he looked at her. 'Will that be a burden? Are you itching to get back to city lights—or something?'

Janie shook her head. A burden? It was a reprieve.

Nell left her wheel and crossed the room to Peter. Without so much as a glance at Lance she said, 'If I had any say in the matter she'd be here for ever. Now, then—tell me how you are. How did you get here? Can you drive a car?'

'Not yet. I'm staying the night with Sid Brown. He drove me here and will be back in a short time. He's told me about Janie,' he added, his eyes returning to her face.

Lance spoke to Maud. 'Could we have coffee? The papers to be signed will take only a few moments.'

He then took Peter to his office, and when they returned Maud poured the coffee. They sat chatting until Sid Brown arrived. However, it was not until after the two men had departed that Penelope returned to the room.

'Peter doesn't look too bad,' she said lightly.

'I thought he looked pale and tired,' Maud said.

Penelope ignored the remark as she looked at Lance. 'Do you think he'll be back at work soon?' she asked hopefully.

He shrugged. 'That's something you yourself could have asked him. You could have put the question while you apologised for your son's behaviour.'

Her manner became defensive. 'What do you mean?'

Lance's voice became hard. 'Do you imagine I don't know about the part young Sam played in Peter's accident? When I visited him in hospital he told me exactly what had happened.'

'Oh.' She looked at him uncertaintly.

'It's my guess that you, also, have known about the struggle at the top of the stairs. I've been waiting for you to admit to the boy's involvement in the affair.'

An expression of defiance crossed her face. 'He's my son—my little boy. It's my duty to protect him.'

'It's your duty to teach him discipline, good manners and obedience—otherwise he'll be a pest to society.'

'But don't you see? He must be allowed to *express* himself.'

'We can see, all right. We can see how well he expressed himself with Peter Bryant. There are limits, you know,' pointed out Lance in a hard and unrelenting tone.

Her eyes reflected pathos as she snatched at the opportunity to beg for help, and despite the presence of the others she said, 'Lance, dear—I must admit he's getting quite beyond me. I'm finding I really can't cope with him. He needs a father—someone like you. Oh, how I *wish you'd be his father*——'

The silence that followed her words was broken by Maud, who spoke in a voice faintly tinged with sarcasm. 'Nell, my dear—I think that Penelope is about to propose to Lance. Perhaps we should go to bed and let her get on with it.'

Neither Lance nor Penelope uttered a word. They just stood and looked at each other, Penelope's face wearing a smile while Lance's expression had become inscrutable.

Maud glanced across the room towards Janie. 'You must be feeling tired, too——'

Janie took the hint to follow them, but paused beside Lance before she reached the door. Her eyes were shadowed by a sense of loss as they gazed up at him. 'I—I hope you'll be happy, Lance,' she felt compelled to say.

'Thank you, Blue-eyes. I'm sure I shall be—when the time comes,' he told her in his deep voice. 'Penelope and I must have a serious talk—do you understand?'

'Of course she understands.' Penelope gave a small laugh that echoed triumph. 'She knows we're going to be married.'

Janie did not wait to hear anything further. Blinded by tears, she left the room and groped her way up the stairs, almost stumbling as she went towards her bedroom. She undressed slowly, her mind filled with the couple downstairs, and the knowledge that any hopes she may have had of winning Lance's love were now dead. As she lay in the darkness, her tears soaked into the pillow.

During the night, her sleep was broken when more tears fell, and in the morning she felt dull and listless. The sun shone brightly, but did little to cheer her as she made her way to the stable where the four horses were already in the yard. Lance, who had preceded her as usual, was busily saddling Major.

He looked at her critically. 'Good morning, Blue-eyes. Dare I say you look somewhat heavy-eyed? Didn't you sleep well?'

She had no wish to discuss her lack of sleep. 'I've had better nights,' was all she admitted.

'What was the trouble?'

'I don't think you'd be interested.'

'Suppose you let me be the judge of that?'

She evaded the question, by asking in a dull voice, 'I presume congratulations are due this morning?'

The dark brows shot up. 'Congratulations? What on earth for?'

'Your engagement, of course. Aren't you and Penelope to be married? I suppose it'll be soon.'

'Don't be stupid!' he snapped.

She turned to stare at him. 'But I thought——'

'You thought matters had come to a head last night?' He left Major and came to stand beside her. 'Is that why you were weeping? Don't try to deny the tears—I can see you've wept for half the night. Those rings round your eyes are telltale.'

Flushing, she turned away to become busy with Gay's girth.

'Was it because you thought Penelope and I were becoming engaged?' he pursued. 'Perhaps I'd better explain what happened.'

Her chin rose a fraction. 'The romantic situation between you and Penelope is not my concern.'

'Isn't it, Blue-eyes? You're sure of that?'

'Quite,' she lied.

'Nevertheless, I want to assure you that the situation between Penelope and myself is not romantic.'

His words surprised her, causing her to turn and look at him.

His eyes held hers in silence as he appeared to ponder a question, and at last he said, 'Normally I wouldn't discuss this matter with anyone, but I think the position should be made clear to you.'

'Why?' she asked in a low voice.

'Because of the tears you shed in the night.'

'They were only because I—I don't think she's the right person for you,' she said as an excuse for her emotions.

'Oh, well—perhaps you wouldn't really be interested——'

'You mean, about the situation between you and Penelope? Of course I'd be interested. Please tell me.'

He grinned. 'I believe you mean it. Well, it was Maud who gave Pen her cue. The moment you'd all left the room she took the bull by the horns. She embraced me and said she thought we should get married.'

'She really *did* propose to you?' Janie asked in a hushed voice.

'Yes. I removed her arms as gently as possible, while I explained that the only woman I'd marry would be one I loved very deeply. She then went on about friendship turning to love, but I explained that that wasn't good enough for me. Didn't I tell you I was about to have a serious talk with her? Well, that was it.'

'She took it calmly?'

'She had little option. She knows me too well to imagine I'd put up with hysterics, ranting and raving. I merely pointed out that if she persisted with the idea of marriage, the longstanding friendship between us would come to an abrupt end. I think she got the message, because the evening ended amicably with another cup of coffee.'

'She *had* missed out on the first one,' Janie reminded him.

'Yes, she slithered out of sight when Peter arrived.' He

turned to face her. 'You're happy to carry on until he's fit for work?'

'Oh, yes—just how happy you'll never know,' she smiled, quite unaware of the inner joy shining through her eyes.

'Thank you, Janie.' He bent and kissed her swiftly, then his arms snatched her body to hold it against his own.

She became conscious of his leaping desire, and as his lips trailed across her face she whispered nervously, 'Somebody might see us. We're in full view of the house——'

'Does it matter?' he murmured against her lips. 'They know I'm grateful to have you here.'

Of course. *Gratitude*—that's all it was. He'd recently escaped the clutches of one woman, therefore he was unlikely to become involved with another. At least, not quite so soon. She sighed inwardly as some of her previous joy slid away, and, disengaging herself from his arms, she said, 'We'd better get on with the job.'

He looked down at her. 'Does that mean you'd rather ride a horse than be held in my arms?'

'That's a stupid question!' she retorted crossly.

'Why? It's something I would like to know.'

'Because if I tell you I'd rather be in your arms, you'd point out that the ponies are waiting to be exercised. You can't fool me, Lance Winter—these ponies are your first love.'

'You honestly believe that?'

'I do,' she told him seriously. 'The only reason your arms go round me is because I'm good with your ponies—and—and not because you have any love for me or—or anything like that——'

An inscrutable expression seemed to darken his eyes, but she went on relentlessly as pent up emotions put words into her mouth.' And let me tell you something else—if Penelope had been good with the ponies—if she'd had *hands*—you'd have married her ages ago.'

He looked at her with sudden perception. 'Is it possible

you've been jealous of Penelope?'

Her voice rose to an angry pitch. '*Jealous?* Huh. You've got to be joking——'

'Then tell me the truth. Why did you spend half the night in tears? Or was it the whole night?'

'That's my business,' she choked.

'I think it's also mine.'

Further words were lost as he snatched her to him again, the force of his arms almost knocking the breath from her. His mouth found hers, his lips moving sensuously as he crushed her against his body. One hand found her breast and held it firmly while his thumb caressed her nipple until flames of desire flared within her.

'Doesn't this tell you anything?' he murmured.

It did. It told her he longed to make love—but it did not tell her that he actually loved her. *Words* were necessary for that sort of commitment, but words of love never passed his lips. Realising this fact, she fought the urge to respond by wrenching her mouth from his and by pushing against his chest. 'The ponies are waiting,' she gasped, and the next moment she was in Gay's saddle.

The rest of the morning passed hazily, while the usual exercises at the poles and on the long, sloping hillside helped to put Janie's mind back on to an even keel. Little was said during the period, although the silences between them veered more towards companionship rather than to anything of an emotional nature.

They were on the long slope when Lance said, 'I'll not be with you this afternoon. I'm taking Sid and Don to see about a mare.'

She was filled by disappointment, but hid it by saying, 'I'll take the horses down to the beach.'

He turned to smile at her. 'Do you think you'll miss me?'

The question surprised her, but she parried it by asking, 'Why should I do that?'

'Because the beach is a lonely place without one's mate.'

'*Mate?*' She looked at him in dismay then fell silent. So there it was. He looked upon her as a mate and nothing more, she realised with a tinge of bitterness.

When they returned to the homestead for lunch, Penelope was distantly polite. 'I'm leaving this afternoon,' she informed Lance. 'Mother says she needs me at home.'

'I understand,' he said without further comment.

Janie looked down at her plate, relieved to know that this would be the last meal when Penelope's dark eyes would become watchful in their effort to probe the situation between Lance and herself. Not that there had been anything for her to observe or learn.

Later, she knew the truth of his earlier words. It *was* lonely on the beach, and today she seemed to miss him more than usual. To help pass the time she tried to remember the lines of poems learnt at school, sang songs to herself and talked to the horses, which she took to the sands singly instead of in pairs.

Major was the last to be given a splash along the edge of the waves, and as she rode Lance's favourite gelding back towards the stable she felt light-hearted with the knowledge that Penelope would have now left for her parents' home.

But Penelope had not departed, and as Janie reached the stable yard she was amazed to discover the tall, dark-haired woman waiting for her. 'Where's Sam?' she demanded, displaying the irritation of one who had been kept waiting.

Janie looked down at her. 'How would I know?'

'He went with you.' Penelope declared crossly.

'He did not.'

'Don't lie to me, Janine Meredith. He said he was going to ride with you—heaven alone knows *why*—and off he went. I watched him go towards the woolshed.'

Janie's voice became cold. 'As usual, your attitude is rude and arrogant, Penelope. Why should I lie to you?'

'Because you hate me—because you're afraid I'll take Lance from you. I *know* you're in love with him.'

Janie flushed. 'What gives you that idea?'

'Don't be stupid, girl. It's written all over your face. It shines out of your eyes—although I never expected to see him fall for a pair of *blue blobs*,' she added furiously.

Janie gave a mirthless laugh. 'You're raving, Penelope. Lance hasn't fallen for me, as you put it.'

'You're sure of that?' New hope crossed the other's face.

'Positive. You're probably over-anxious about Sam.'

'Then where is he? He went ages ago. You must have seen him.'

'For your information, I've spent the afternoon on the beach and nowhere near the direction in which he seems to have ridden.'

'*Then go and find him!*' The order was almost shouted.

Janie looked at her in icy silence.

'If not, get off that horse and I'll go—although Lance will be furious when he knows I've been riding his precious Major.'

Janie realised that Lance would also be furious if he knew she'd handed Major over to someone who didn't have *hands*, and even as she hesitated Penelope's attitude took on a sudden change.

'Please, Janie,' she pleaded. 'That new pony is proving to be unpredictable. Sam could have been thrown.'

It was enough for Janie. There had been times when she herself had wondered about Rainbow, and now she ceased to hesitate. The thought of Sam lying on one of the hillsides sent her cantering along the farm road, beyond the woolshed and past the haybarn. As her eyes scanned the sloping pastures, her concern for Sam's safety grew.

She had no idea what sent her towards the boundary fence. The last time she had followed its line she had been with Lance, and they had come to where Don had been moving a stretch of it away from the cliff edge. Now, as she approached that same area, she saw Rainbow tethered to the fence, although there was no sign of Sam.

As she drew near she became aware of two Cape pigeons wheeling in circles beyond the edge of the cliff, their harsh, shrieking cackles indicating agitation. She dismounted beside Rainbow, looked about her and shouted loudly, 'Sam! Sam! Where are you?'

A faint sobbing voice came to her ears. 'I'm here—I can't get up. Come and help me——'

Fear shot through her as she realised the voice came from over the cliff. She tethered Major to a post, then climbed the fence and peered over the edge.

Sam was on a ledge that was little more than a few feet in width and a short distance below her. To the left of him, but just out of his reach, a craggy niche in the steep slope of the cliff wall held a Cape pigeon's nest with one white egg.

His face was pale and tear-stained as he gazed up at her. 'Why didn't you come and find me sooner?' he complained unreasonably. 'I've been here for ages and ages——'

'You silly boy. What on earth are you doing down there?'

'I looked over the edge to see where Uncle Lance's father fell—and then I saw that nest. I thought I could get it.'

'So you slid down the slope to steal the egg, and now you can't get up because it's too steep.'

'I've tried and tried,' he wept. 'I keep slipping back.'

'Didn't you think about getting back when you went down?'

'No, I just wanted the egg. Janie, those birds are squawking at me. I'm afraid they'll peck me. Get me up from here!'

Lying on the ground, she reached down towards him but, although she could clasp his upstretched hands, she did not have the strength to pull him to the higher level.

Sam looked up at her hopefully. 'If you get down here and lift me, I could put my foot on a big stone that's sticking out of the cliff. Then I could reach the tufts growing along the top edge.'

'But if I can't lift you high enough we'd both be stuck

down there,' she pointed out, trying to keep her eyes and mind from the drop beyond the ledge. The thought of Lance's father made her feel ill. Telling herself that control of thought was necessary, she tried to concentrate on the problem of getting the boy up.

At last she said, 'Sam, I'll try to pull you up. I'll fetch Major's surcingle.'

Scrambling to her feet, she hurried back to the horse, where she removed not only the surcingle but also the stirrup leathers. The end of the surcingle was slipped through its own buckle to form a loop that could be drawn into a noose, and then the added stirrup leathers gave extra length.

As she lowered the end over the edge towards Sam, she said, 'Place the loop over your head and beneath your arms, then pull it as tight as you can.'

'Yeah, OK. I've done that——' he called after a pause.

'While I'm pulling, you must try to claw your way up.'

But although she pulled with all her strength little progress was made, making her fear the task would prove to be beyond her.

'I keep slipping back,' Sam yelled. '*Pull harder!*'

'I'm doing my best,' she gasped, fighting the feeling of desperation that was beginning to grip her. Her legs trembled as she tried to dig her heels into the firm ground, but they gained no hold on the slippery grass, and she kept sliding forward. Her arms felt as though they were being dragged from their sockets—her hands burned as they grasped the hard leather.

The struggle seemed hopeless, as uncontrolled gasps left her lungs and tears from the pain in her hands and arms stung her eyes. She knew her strength was waning, and her vision blurred as a frantic pull brought a yell from Sam.

'I've got my foot on the stone—I can reach the tufts— pull *harder—harder*———'

Sobs were escaping her, as she feared she hadn't the

strength for the final effort, but suddenly there was a pounding of hoofs in her ears, then a squeaking of wires as somebody climbed the fence behind her. In the next instant, Lance's hands gripped the leather, to pull Sam over the top.

Janie collapsed on the ground, her body shaking while tears ran down her face. Her head swam and her ears buzzed as she heard Sam's voice telling Lance about his great adventure.

'You see, there was this egg in the nest. I went down to get it, but I couldn't reach it—and then I couldn't get up. But Janie—she got me up—well, *nearly*——'

Lance cut him short. 'You will get on that pony and ride home *at once*!' he ordered crisply. 'Your mother is waiting for you. I'll have a good talk to you later. Now, then—*get going*!'

'Yeah—OK. Thank for helping me, Janie. Gosh—what are you crying for? I'm all right, aren't I? I didn't fall over the edge—the birds didn't peck at me——'

'*Go—go*——!' Lance roared.

A squeak of wires, and then movement from Rainbow, told Janie the boy had departed, but she continued to lie on the grass, her body still shaken by sobs although she knew that Lance was now kneeling beside her.

'Have a good weep,' he advised gently. 'Wash it out of your system.' His hand stroked her golden hair.

'I'm sorry for being such an idiot,' she gasped as a fresh bout of trembling shook her. 'I suppose it's reaction.'

'Of course it is—so just let the tears flow.'

'I was so afraid I wouldn't be able to hold him—that he'd fall and roll over the edge. If you hadn't come to take the burden——'

He changed to a sitting position, then lifted her from the ground to hold her across his lap and against his chest. Looking down into her face, he said, 'My darling, from now on I'll bear all your burdens. Do you understand?'

She gazed up at him, wondering if she'd imagined the

endearment. 'Wh-what do you mean?'

'I mean that I want you beside me for as long as we can have together.'

Her eyes widened as she found difficulty in believing her ears. 'You—you do?'

'I love you, Janie.' The words came simply. 'I think you love me, too. At least, I'm hoping you do.'

She nodded, unable to speak, and fearing that this was nothing more than hallucination—a dream of wishful thinking.

His arms tightened about her as he lowered his face to find her lips. 'Then you'll marry me, my dearest?'

'Yes—yes——'

'Then tell me you love me.'

She clung to him, her voice ringing with sincerity. 'I love you, Lance Winter. I've loved you for—for ages.'

'And I've loved you from the first day you stepped into the living-room. You sat beside me on the window seat. The sun shining through your hair gave you a halo that made you look like an angel.'

She was surprised. 'Since then? You kept it well hidden.'

'I fought against it, except for odd moments when it almost got out of hand.'

'Moments like those in the hayloft?' she prompted shyly.

He changed his position so that he lay beside her on the grass, his body half covering hers. 'The hayloft was not the right place,' he admitted softly. 'At least—I could think of a better place.'

She became conscious of his pulsating desire. 'Surely you're not suggesting it should be at the edge of a cliff?'

A quiet laugh escaped him as he shook his head. 'No, I want you in our own bed, my darling—naked and free. I've been driven crazy for long enough, knowing you were only in the next room, but I can still wait. When can we be married?'

She looked up to gaze upon the tender love shining from

his eyes. It was an expression she had never seen before, and now the sight of it filled her with quiet happiness. 'Let's make it as soon as possible,' she whispered.

He held her against him, his hands massaging her back as he pressed her to his body. 'You're feeling better,' he observed with satisfaction. 'You've stopped trembling.'

'You've pushed the nightmare out of my mind,' she sighed.

'My poor darling—you had nowhere to turn for help.'

'No. I knew you were away somewhere with Sid and Don, but you did get here in time.' She looked at him pleadingly. 'Darling, can we please leave this place?'

He helped her to her feet and they climbed the fence. He replaced Major's surcingle and stirrups, then assisted her to mount.

She looked down at him. 'Are you sure you wouldn't rather ride Major?'

'Of course not. I'm happy on Dandy, and I like to see you on Major. Soon we'll be really sharing him.'

His words seemed to make this dream situation more real, although she remained in a happy daze as they rode back towards the homestead. At times, she imagined she saw a secretive smile playing about his lips and, while she wondered about it vaguely, she did not ask why it should be there or what amused him.

However, the answer to its existence came as they approached the paddock surrounding the stable, and her attention was caught by the sight of an extra horse grazing beside Gay and Joy. It was a black mare. She drew rein to stare at it incredulously. '*That's my Topsy!*' she almost shrieked with delight.

'Yes. I thought you'd like to have her here.'

'It was Topsy you went to see this afternoon with Sid and Don?'

'That's right. That's why we weren't here when you needed us.'

But happiness had now brushed that episode from her mind. She whistled loudly. The mare raised her head, then came towards them.

Lance said, 'Well, I'll be darned! This afternoon it took nearly half an hour for the three of us to catch her.'

Janie dismounted, and then tears filled her eyes as she fondled the velvety nose. 'Thank you, Lance—oh, darling—thank you.'

Later, as they walked into the living-room, they found Nell at her spinning. The small woman took one look at Janie's radiant face, then left her wheel to come and clasp her hand. 'Something has happened?' she asked hesitantly.

Lance put his arms about Janie. 'It sure has, little Nell.'

'I *knew* it!' Nell exclaimed on a note of triumph. 'The moment Sid Brown told me they'd brought home a black mare belonging to Janie— *I knew it*. Otherwise, why would Lance bring it here? Maud, didn't I tell you so?'

Maud came from the kitchen area. 'You certainly did,' she agreed, as she expressed her delight by hugging them both. Then, being ever practical, she turned to Janie. 'You'd better phone your mother at once. She'll want to know about having a wedding on her hands——'

'And tell her we'll see her tomorrow,' Lance added. 'We'll go to Napier to buy a ring. If memory serves me corectly, it's a cluster sitting on the shelf below the Rock of Gibraltar.'

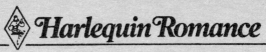 **Harlequin Romance**

Coming Next Month

Temptation ™

TEMPTATION WILL BE
EVEN HARDER TO RESIST...

In September, Temptation is presenting a sophisticated new face to the world. A fresh look that truly brings Harlequin's most intimate romances into focus.

What's more, all-time favorite authors Barbara Delinsky, Rita Clay Estrada, Jayne Ann Krentz and Vicki Lewis Thompson will join forces to help us celebrate. The result? A very special quartet of Temptations...

- **Four striking covers**
- **Four stellar authors**
- **Four sensual love stories**
- **Four variations on one spellbinding theme**

All in one great month! Give in to Temptation in September.

TDESIGN-1

Harlequin Superromance

**Here are the longer, more involving stories you
have been waiting for...Superromance.**

Modern, believable novels of love, full of the complex
joys and heartaches of real people.

Intriguing conflicts based on today's constantly
changing life-styles.

Four new titles every month.
Available wherever paperbacks are sold.

SUPER-1

ATTRACTIVE, SPACE SAVING BOOK RACK

Display your most prized novels on this handsome and sturdy book rack. The hand-rubbed walnut finish will blend into your library decor with quiet elegance, providing a practical organizer for your favorite hard-or soft-covered books.

Only $9.95

Approximately 16" x 8" when assembled

Assembles in seconds!

To order, rush your name, address and zip code, along with a check or money order for $10.70* ($9.95 plus 75¢ postage and handling) payable to *Harlequin Reader Service*:

Harlequin Reader Service
Book Rack Offer
901 Fuhrmann Blvd.
P.O. Box 1396
Buffalo, NY 14269-1396

Offer not available in Canada.

BKR-1A

*New York and Iowa residents add appropriate sales tax.

HARLEQUIN SIGNATURE EDITION

VIOLET WINSPEAR

HOUSE OF STORMS

Editorial secretary Debra Hartway travels to the Salvador family's rugged Cornish island home to work on Jack Salvador's latest book. Disturbing questions hang in the troubled air over Lovelis Island. What or who had caused the tragic death of Jack's young wife? Why did Jack stay away from the home and, more especially, the baby son he loved so well? And—why should Rodare, Jack's brother, who had proved himself a man of the highest integrity, constantly invade Debra's thoughts with such passionate, dark desires...?

Violet Winspear, who has written more than 65 romance novels translated worldwide into 18 languages, is one of Harlequin's best-loved and bestselling authors. HOUSE OF STORMS, her second title in the Harlequin Signature Edition program, is a full-length novel rich in romantic tradition and intriguingly spiced with an atmosphere of danger and mystery.

Watch for HOUSE OF STORMS—coming in October!   HOFS-1